FRAMING THE AUTHOR

GARY B

For permissions, inquiries, or more about the author, visit:
www.amazon.com/stores/Gary-B/author/B0F83JMYBY

First Edition: July 2025

CHAPTER 1: THROUGH THE GLASS

The cursor blinked. Mockingly. Rhythmically. Each flash like the steady beat of a metronome counting the seconds of Daniel Mercer's mounting failure. The white document remained pristine, untouched by a single word for the past three hours and forty-seven minutes. Daniel knew this because he'd been staring at the time stamp in the corner of his screen, watching minutes dissolve into hours as his deadline loomed ever closer.

Three bestsellers in five years had earned him this corner office in his Brooklyn brownstone. It was a room with tall windows that bathed his antique writing desk in natural light. The space that had once felt sacred now felt like a prison cell. The bookshelves lining the walls displayed his previous works, their spines aligned perfectly, each one a reminder of expectations he feared he could no longer meet.

Daniel ran his fingers through his salt-and-pepper hair, noticing more silver strands than he remembered from last week. At forty-two, the wrinkles at the corners of his eyes had deepened considerably in the eighteen months since his last book hit the shelves. Eighteen months of false starts and deleted drafts. Eighteen months of his agent's increasingly terse emails. Eighteen months of his publisher's thinly veiled threats about contract obligations.

"Goddamnit," he muttered, pushing away from his desk with enough force to send his ergonomic chair rolling back against the bookcase. The impact dislodged a framed review from The New York Times that had once proclaimed him "the new master of literary suspense." The glass cracked as it hit the hardwood floor.

Perfect. A fitting metaphor for his career trajectory.

Daniel stood and crossed to the window, pressing his forehead against the cool glass. October had painted the neighborhood trees in vivid reds and yellows, a stark contrast to the gray fog of his imagination. He'd always loved autumn in New York, the crisp air, the scent of cinnamon and spice wafting from the café down the street, the upcoming chill in the air. All of it had once sparked his creativity. Now, nothing.

The routine had become his prison. Wake at six, black coffee, no sugar. Sit at the same mahogany desk his father had left him. Open the laptop. Stare at the cursor blinking mockingly on the blank page.

By noon, he'd managed maybe three sentences, all destined for deletion. Lunch was always the same turkey sandwich, eaten standing over the kitchen sink while he scrolled through social media, watching other authors celebrate their latest deals, their glowing reviews, their literary prizes.

The afternoons were worse. He'd tried everything; changing locations, writing by hand, dictating into his phone during long walks through Central Park. He'd bought expensive pens, lucky notebooks, even a vintage typewriter that now sat gathering dust in the corner like an accusation. The sound of its keys had once thrilled him; now it reminded him of everything he couldn't produce.

His editor had suggested therapy. "Writer's block is just fear," she'd said during their last lunch meeting, her voice carrying that particular blend of sympathy and impatience reserved for underperforming assets.

"What are you afraid of, Daniel?"

Everything, he'd wanted to say. Afraid that his previous novel's success had been a fluke. Afraid that he'd used up all his stories, that the well had run dry at forty-two. Afraid that the critics who'd once praised his "unflinching psychological insight" would tear apart whatever he managed to produce next. Afraid that he was becoming irrelevant in a world that moved faster than he could think.

The apartment felt smaller each day, its silence oppressive. He'd grown used to talking to himself, sometimes reading old passages aloud just to hear words that weren't trapped in his head. The cleaning lady, Rosa, had started giving him concerned looks when she came twice a week. Last Tuesday, she'd asked if he was eating enough, her weathered hands gesturing at his increasingly hollow cheeks.

He wasn't sleeping well either. Three, maybe four hours a night, and those filled with dreams about empty pages and disappointed faces. He'd taken to working through the night sometimes, convinced that exhaustion might break through whatever wall had built itself around his imagination. It never worked, but the ritual of failure had become as familiar as breathing.

Daniel's phone buzzed against the desk; probably another "checking in" text from his agent or a reminder about an upcoming deadline he couldn't possibly meet. He didn't look. Instead, he pressed harder against the window, watching his breath fog the glass, when movement in the apartment across the courtyard caught his eye.

A moving truck was parked in front of the building across the street, and movers were carrying furniture inside. The brownstone directly opposite his had been vacant for months after the elderly couple who'd lived there for decades had finally relocated to Florida. Daniel watched with mild interest as the movers unloaded sleek, contemporary furniture, nothing like the antique pieces the previous owners had cherished.

A woman appeared on the stoop, gesturing animatedly to the movers. Even from this distance, Daniel could see she was striking, tall with dark hair cut in a sharp bob that framed a face with pronounced cheekbones. She wore a fitted black turtleneck and dark jeans, an outfit that seemed both casual and meticulously chosen. There was something captivating about her presence, the way she commanded attention without seeming to try.

A small notepad lay on the windowsill where Daniel sometimes jotted ideas while looking out at the street. He picked it up, his fingers tingling slightly as they wrapped around the pen beside it. Without thinking, he began to sketch a rough character profile:

New neighbor. 30s? Confident posture. Precise movements. Everything deliberate. What's her story? Divorced? Starting over? Running from something? Professional, doctor? Lawyer? Gallery owner? Someone with power and control. Someone who requires a mask.

The words flowed effortlessly for the first time in months. Daniel felt a small spark, like the fire that had once burned within him when developing characters. He continued watching as the woman supervised the placement of a large abstract painting on her living room wall, visible through her uncurtained windows. Who moves in and immediately hangs art before the boxes are even unpacked?

Someone who values appearances. Someone who needs the world they present to be perfectly curated.

Daniel's phone vibrated on his desk, his agent, Patricia, calling for the third time that day. He let it go to voicemail. Instead, he pulled up a chair to the window and continued observing. The woman moved through her new space with purpose, directing movers with precision, occasionally checking her watch.

At one point, she looked up suddenly, her gaze seeming to fix directly on Daniel's window. He instinctively stepped back, heart racing as if he'd been caught trespassing, though he knew logically that the afternoon sun would be reflecting off his windows, making it impossible for her to see inside.

Still, her gaze lingered long enough to send a chill down his spine before she turned away to sign something on the movers' clipboard.

Hours passed. Daniel remained at the window, watching as the moving truck departed and his new neighbor began the methodical process of unpacking. As dusk fell, lights flickered on in her apartment, creating perfect visibility into her living space. She hadn't hung curtains yet, why would she? The brownstones were set far enough apart that privacy was rarely a concern, and most residents relied on an unspoken agreement not to look too closely into neighbors' windows.

An agreement Daniel was now blatantly violating.

Darkness fell completely outside, transforming his window into a mirror that reflected his gaunt face back at him. He looked away from his own reflection and focused instead on the illuminated tableau across the street.

The woman had changed into loose-fitting silk pajamas and poured herself a glass of red wine. She moved to a sleek black piano that the movers had positioned near her own window and began to play, her fingers dancing across the keys with practiced ease.

Daniel couldn't hear the music from his position, but he could see the passion in her movements, the slight sway of her body as she played. This wasn't casual playing; this was expertise, perhaps even professional training. He added that detail to his growing notes.

For the first time in eighteen months, he felt the familiar itch in his fingertips, the compulsion to write. Not just any story, but her story, or rather, a version of it woven with the same threads of suspense that had made his previous novels so successful.

Daniel returned to his desk, the blank document no longer an accusation but an invitation. The cursor still blinked, but now its rhythm felt like anticipation rather than condemnation. His fingers hovered over the keyboard for just a moment before he began to type:

Lila didn't believe in coincidences. When she first saw him watching her through the window, she knew it wasn't by chance. It was exactly what she had been waiting for, exactly what she had planned.

The words poured out of him, fueled by the mysterious woman across the street. Daniel wrote until the early hours of the morning, stopping only when he noticed the lights in her apartment had finally gone dark. He had written seventeen pages, more than he'd accomplished in months. The main character in his new thriller was taking shape, inspired by but not identical to his new neighbor. In his story, she was Lila Blackwood, a concert pianist with a dark past who had carefully selected her new home for a very specific purpose.

As Daniel finally powered down his laptop and prepared for bed, he glanced one last time at the darkened windows across the street. A strange sense of gratitude mingled with unease settled in his stomach. He had found his muse, but at what cost to his conscience.

Sleep came quickly but brought troubling dreams: the woman at the piano, her eyes suddenly meeting his through both their windows, her lips curving into a knowing smile as she mouthed words he couldn't hear but somehow understood:

I see you too

CHAPTER 2: REFLECTIONS

Daniel woke to sunlight streaming through his bedroom window. For the first time in months, he didn't feel the immediate weight of dread pressing against his chest. Instead, a peculiar energy coursed through him, the residual buzz of creative flow. He reached for his phone: 10:47 AM. He'd slept later than usual, his body compensating for the late-night writing session.

Three missed calls from Patricia, two text messages asking if he was still alive. And an email from his publisher with the subject line: "FINAL DEADLINE EXTENSION - NOT NEGOTIABLE." Daniel ignored them all. He had something now, something real taking shape.

After a quick shower, he made his way to the kitchen, brewing coffee strong enough to strip paint. The scent filled his apartment, earthy and rich, a reminder of the creative momentum humming through his veins. Cup in hand, he wandered back to his office, unable to resist checking across the street.

The woman's apartment looked different in daylight, more ordinary, less mysterious. But still, something about it nagged at him. Everything seemed too perfect, too deliberately arranged. Who unpacks and decorates so completely in a single afternoon? The books on her shelves were organized by color, creating an ombré effect that looked more like a magazine spread than a lived-in home.

His attention was rewarded when she appeared, dressed in fitted black athletic wear, her dark bob tucked behind her ears. She moved to the center of her living room, rolled out a yoga mat, and began a series of fluid movements. Not casual stretching, this was advanced yoga, poses flowing into one another with a dancer's precision. Daniel watched, mesmerized by her control and strength, the way she held difficult positions with apparent ease.

He should feel guilty about watching. He knew this. But the writer in him, that part that had been dormant for so long rationalized that this was research. Character study. Creative necessity.

His laptop beckoned. Daniel settled at his desk, positioned so he could glance up occasionally at his unwitting muse, and began to read through what he'd written the previous night. The words were good, better than good. The narrative voice had a confidence he hadn't felt in years. His fictional creation, Lila Blackwood, was taking shape as a complex character. She was brilliant, disciplined, harboring secrets that drove her every careful move. Her every decision was towards her goal and secrecy was very important.

Daniel's fingers found the keyboard again, continuing where he'd left off:

Lila knew the power of routine, how establishing predictable patterns could disarm observers, make her seem transparent when she was anything but. Each morning's ritual was another brushstroke in the portrait she presented to the world: dedicated, health-conscious, ordinary. Nothing to suggest the elaborate mechanism ticking away beneath her practiced serenity.

He paused, looking up to see his neighbor concluding her yoga routine with a perfect headstand. As she held the inverted position, her gaze drifted toward his window. Daniel froze, though he knew he was probably invisible to her. After a long moment, she lowered herself gracefully to the mat and rolled it up, disappearing into another room.

Daniel released a breath he hadn't realized he was holding, scared to his roots. He returned to writing, allowing his imagination to fill in the gaps of her life, creating a backstory for his fictional Lila that grew darker with each paragraph.

In his story, she was a renowned pianist whose career had been derailed by a scandal, a violent incident involving a former lover who had threatened to expose her fraudulent past. His Lila had reinvented herself multiple times, each identity more carefully constructed than the last.

Two hours passed in what felt like minutes. When Daniel finally paused, his wrists aching pleasantly from sustained typing, he had added another twenty pages to his manuscript. The neighbor had long since disappeared from view, but her presence lingered in his imagination, fueling this creative resurrection.

His phone rang again, Patricia, predictably. This time, he answered.

"You're alive," she said, her voice sharp with relief and irritation. "I was about to send a welfare check to your apartment."

"I'm fine," Daniel replied, surprised by the lightness in his own voice. "Better than fine, actually. I'm writing."

A beat of silence. "Really writing? Or just telling me that to get me off your back?"

"Really writing. Something new. It's..." he hesitated, unsure how to explain without sounding unhinged. "It's flowing, Pat. I think this one is different."

"Thank God," she sighed. "The publisher's ready to invoke the contract clause, Dan. They want their advance back if you don't deliver something by the end of the month." The familiar anxiety flickered, but didn't take hold.

"I'll have something. Not the whole manuscript, but enough to show them I'm back on track."

"What's it about?" Patricia asked, the literary agent in her immediately taking precedence over her concern for his well-being.

Daniel gazed out the window. "A psychological thriller. A woman with a carefully constructed life and the man who becomes obsessed with uncovering her secrets." He paused. "It's about perception, and how we never really know what's happening behind closed doors."

"Sounds on-brand for you," Patricia said. "Send me the first fifty pages when you have them. And Daniel, don't disappear again. I mean it."

After promising to stay in touch, Daniel ended the call and returned to the window. The apartment across the street remained empty, its occupant elsewhere. For a moment, he wondered where she might have gone. To work? What did she do? Where had she come from?

He was contemplating these questions when something caught his eye, not in her apartment, but on the street below. His neighbor was returning, shopping bags in hand. From his vantage point, Daniel could see her clearly: sunglasses perched on her head, that same purposeful stride. As she climbed the steps to her building, she paused and looked up, directly at his window, it seemed, before disappearing inside.

Daniel stepped back, heart racing again. Coincidence, he told himself. She couldn't possibly know he'd been watching her. Couldn't know she'd become the template for his fictional creation.

He returned to his desk, but found his focus disturbed. On impulse, he opened his browser and typed: "how to research someone without their knowledge." The search results made him flinch, articles about stalking, privacy laws, ethical boundaries. He closed the tab quickly, ashamed.

But the writer's voice in his head persisted: *You need to know more. For the book. For authenticity.*

That evening, as dusk gathered, Daniel ordered takeout from the Thai restaurant down the block, the same one he'd watched his neighbor call earlier, her delivery arriving thirty minutes before he placed his own order. He told himself this was just an odd coincidence, but part of him wanted to establish a connection, however tenuous, to her daily rhythms.

When the delivery person arrived, Daniel overtipped and asked casually, "Hey, you deliver across the street too, right? To the woman who just moved in?"

The young man nodded. "Yeah, she's a good tipper. Ordered the same thing as you, actually. Pad Thai, extra spicy."

"Really?" Daniel said, trying to sound merely amused by the coincidence. "She must have a good taste."

After the delivery person left, Daniel stood in his darkening apartment, container of Pad Thai in hand, staring across at the now-illuminated windows of his neighbor's home. She sat at her dining table, eating the same meal, reading a book he couldn't identify from this distance.

He took his food to his desk and opened his manuscript, typing with one hand as he ate:

Lila believed in controlling variables. Each calculated choice, from what she ate to what she wore, was another thread in the web she was spinning, waiting for him to stumble into it.

Daniel paused, fork halfway to his mouth. The line he'd just written sent an uncomfortable shiver through him. In his story, who exactly was the predator, and who was the prey?

As if sensing his thoughts, his neighbor suddenly looked up from her book and turned toward her window. This time, instead of quickly looking away, she stood and walked purposefully toward the glass. For a heart-stopping moment, she seemed to stare directly at him, her expression unreadable across the distance. Then, with deliberate slowness, she reached up and drew the curtains closed for the first time since moving in.

Daniel sat motionless, his food forgotten, the cursor blinking steadily on his screen. The message felt unmistakable.

She knew he was watching.

CHAPTER 3: INTERSECTIONS

The closed curtains haunted Daniel for three days. Each morning, he'd find himself drifting to the window, coffee in hand, only to find the fabric still drawn across her windows, a beige barrier between his curiosity and her life. His writing slowed without the visual stimulus, though the momentum hadn't disappeared entirely. The character of Lila had taken root in his imagination, growing independently of her inspiration now. Still, he missed the voyeuristic thrill, the details that had added such authenticity to his prose.

On the fourth morning, Daniel woke to the sound of rain pattering against his windows. October had turned suddenly cold overnight, the wind driving sheets of water against the brownstones. He wrapped himself in his worn flannel robe and padded to the office, expecting to see the same curtains drawn.

Instead, they were open again. The apartment across the street was empty, but showed signs of life returning, a mug on the coffee table, a throw blanket unfolded on the couch. Daniel felt an absurd surge of gratitude, followed immediately by shame. What kind of person was he becoming?

The kind who had written sixty-seven pages in four days after eighteen months of nothing.

He settled at his desk and opened his manuscript, rereading the last few passages he'd written without his visual muse. In his story, Lila Blackwood was methodically inserting herself into the life of her target, a once-successful true crime author whose last book had accused the wrong man of a notorious murder.

Her brother, as Daniel had written, who had committed suicide in prison while awaiting trial. Her elaborate plan for revenge was unfolding with clockwork precision.

The narrative felt electric with tension, even to Daniel himself. But something was missing now, those small, observed details that had made the early pages so vivid.

A movement across the street caught his eye. His neighbor had entered her living room, phone pressed to her ear, gesturing emphatically with her free hand. She looked agitated, pacing in front of her window. Whatever conversation she was having, it wasn't pleasant. Daniel watched as she ran her fingers through her dark hair, disrupting its perfect symmetry for the first time since he'd begun observing her.

He found himself reaching for his notebook, jotting down observations:

Hair disheveled. First sign of genuine emotion. Argument with whom? Lover? Family? Professional crisis? Voice raised; wish I could hear. Keeps checking watch, time pressure?

The woman ended her call abruptly, tossing her phone onto the couch with enough force to suggest anger. She stood motionless for a moment; hands pressed against her face. Then, with what appeared to be a deep breath, she straightened her posture, smoothed her hair, and visibly composed herself. Her transformation was deliberate it was like watching an actor prepare to go onstage.

Daniel's fingers itched to capture this in his manuscript. He began typing rapidly:

Lila's carefully maintained façade cracked only in private, and even then, never for long. She had trained herself to compartmentalize, to tuck away anything that might interfere with her objectives. The call from her former conservatory director threatening to reveal her past had rattled her, but only momentarily. Five seconds of genuine distress, then back into character: collected, controlled, calculating.

He glanced up again to see his neighbor checking her appearance in a mirror, applying lipstick; a deep red that accentuated the pallor of her skin. She gathered a leather portfolio and keys, slipped into a tailored black trench coat, and left her apartment.

An idea formed in Daniel's mind, reckless and compelling. The rain had slowed to a drizzle. If he hurried, he could be at the corner café before she walked by; a seemingly chance encounter that might satisfy his growing need to know more about her. To hear her voice, to observe her up close. For the book, he justified to himself. For authenticity. If she was not headed that way then this opportunity would go waste'

Daniel dressed quickly, choosing clothes more thoughtfully than he had in months. He picked up dark jeans, a gray cashmere sweater that Patricia had given him after his second bestseller, leather boots. He ran a comb through his hair, noticing with surprise that he'd developed shadows under his eyes despite sleeping better than he had in a year.

Five minutes later, he was positioned at a table outside the café, a newspaper open in front of him, an untouched cappuccino steaming in the cool air. The mist clung to everything, wrapping the brownstones in a soft gray haze that blurred edges and muffled sounds. Daniel tried to appear casual, though his heart hammered against his ribs as he waited.

He didn't have to wait long. She appeared at the corner, walking briskly, the collar of her trench coat turned up against the damp. Up close, she was even more striking, high cheekbones, dark eyes framed by lashes that seemed too long to be natural, that sharp bob of black hair now slightly curled from the humidity. She moved with athletic grace, her heels clicking authoritatively against the wet sidewalk.

As she approached the café, Daniel pretended to be absorbed in his newspaper. She paused at the door, so close that he could smell her perfume, something expensive and subtle with notes of amber and spice. The scent triggered a strange sense of déjà vu that he couldn't place.

Just as she was about to enter the café, her portfolio slipped from her grasp, sending papers scattering across the wet pavement.

"Darn it," she muttered, her voice low and melodic despite the frustration.

Daniel saw his opportunity and seized it, jumping up to help gather the wind-blown papers. "Let me help you with that," he said, crouching to collect a sheet that had plastered itself against the café window.

She looked at him directly for the first time, her eyes a startling shade of amber; almost golden in the gray morning light. "Thank you," she said, the words precise and measured.

They gathered the papers together, Daniel careful not to appear too eager or to examine the documents too closely, though he caught glimpses of what looked like architectural drawings and columns of numbers. When the last sheet had been secured, he handed his collection to her with what he hoped was a friendly, neighborly smile.

"Looks important," he commented. "I hope nothing's damaged."

She assessed him for a moment before responding, her gaze so penetrating that Daniel wondered wildly if she recognized him; if somehow she'd been watching him too.

"Nothing irreplaceable," she replied finally. "But valuable, nonetheless. Thank you for your help." She extended her hand. "I'm Mira Voss."

"Daniel Mercer," he said, taking her hand. Her grip was firm, her skin cool from the autumn air. "I think we're neighbors, actually. I live across the street. The brownstone with the blue door."

Something flickered across her expression, recognition? Wariness? It disappeared too quickly for Daniel to interpret. "Yes, I've seen the building," she said. "I just moved in last week." She tilted her head slightly. "Are you *the* Daniel Mercer? The author?"

The question caught him off guard, though it shouldn't have. His photo was on his book jackets, and he'd done enough interviews when his last thriller hit the bestseller lists that recognition wasn't uncommon. Still, the idea that she might have been aware of him before this moment shifted the dynamic in a way that made him uneasy.

"Guilty as charged," he admitted. "Though these days I'm more aspirational than productive."

Mira's lips curved into a smile that didn't quite reach her eyes. "Writer's block? How terribly cliché for someone of your talent."

There was something in her tone, a hint of mockery that raised the hair on Daniel's arms. Before he could respond, she glanced at her watch. "I'm running late for a meeting. Perhaps we'll run into each other again, neighbor. I'd love to hear about your next project sometime."

Without waiting for his response, she entered the café, ordered something from the barista in a voice too low for Daniel to catch, and exited moments later with a to-go cup, disappearing around the corner toward the subway station.

Daniel remained frozen at his table, the encounter replaying in his mind. Mira Voss. The name felt significant somehow, though he was certain he'd never heard it before. And there was something unsettling about the way she'd looked at him; as if she knew something he didn't.

Back in his apartment, Daniel searched for her name online. The results were sparse but intriguing: Mira Voss, 36, an architectural consultant specializing in historical renovations. A professional website with an impressive portfolio but minimal personal information. No social media presence that he could find unusual for someone her age, especially a professional who would presumably benefit from networking.

Most interesting was a brief mention in an article about a controversial renovation project in Boston two years earlier; a historic theater being converted into luxury condominiums. Mira had been the lead consultant, but had withdrawn from the project abruptly after structural issues were discovered. The article hinted at disputes between her and the developers, though details were vague.

Boston. Something about that triggered another wave of déjà vu for Daniel, though he couldn't place why. He'd visited the city several times for book events, but nothing memorable stood out.

Returning to his manuscript, Daniel incorporated elements of their encounter, transforming the brief interaction into a pivotal scene in his thriller. In his version, the protagonist, Marcus recognized Lila immediately as someone connected to the murder case he'd written about years earlier. The characters' awareness of each other added a layer of tension that excited Daniel as he wrote.

Hours passed as he worked, the words flowing seamlessly. Outside, the rain had intensified again, drumming against the windows. Darkness fell early, the streetlights casting golden pools on the wet asphalt. Daniel finally paused, stretching his stiff muscles, and looked across at Mira's apartment.

The curtains were open, the lights on. She sat at her piano again, but wasn't playing. Instead, she appeared to be writing something, her attention focused on papers spread across the piano's glossy surface. Occasionally she would pause, look up as if considering something, then return to her task.

Daniel watched, wondering what kind of architectural project required such intensity after business hours. As if sensing his scrutiny, Mira suddenly looked up, directly at his window, and smiled. A deliberate, knowing smile that sent a chill through him. Then, without breaking her gaze, she slowly gathered her papers into a neat stack, rose from the piano bench, and once again drew the curtains closed.

The message was unmistakable this time. Not only was she aware of his observation—she was playing into it. Daniel turned back to his manuscript, heart racing, and added a new line:

Marcus had made a critical error in his calculations. He'd assumed he was the observer, the one in control of the narrative unfolding between them. But as Lila's eyes met his across the distance, he realized the truth: this wasn't his story at all. It was hers, and had been from the beginning.

That night, Daniel dreamed of amber eyes watching him through darkness, and of music he could see but not hear, the notes floating across the street like silent messengers carrying warnings he couldn't quite understand.

The remaining hours of the day passed with excruciating slowness. Daniel tried to write but found himself distracted, his attention constantly drifting to the closed curtains across the street. Each paragraph required twice the usual effort; his mind preoccupied with the evening ahead rather than the fictional world he was creating. The words that had flowed so effortlessly since he began watching Mira now came in reluctant drips, contaminated by self-consciousness.

By two o'clock, he'd written only three paragraphs, none of which satisfied him. In his story, Marcus was preparing to confront Lila at a gallery opening, a public setting where both would be forced to maintain their facades. Daniel deleted the scene entirely. It felt contrived now, a pale imitation of the real confrontation awaiting him across the street.

At three, he gave up on writing entirely and wandered restlessly through his apartment. He paused at each window, though only the office provided a view of Mira's building. The apartment felt suddenly claustrophobic, the walls too close, the air too still. He opened a window despite the chill, letting the damp October breeze cleanse the staleness.

CHAPTER 4: MANUSCRIPT

The email from Patricia arrived at 7:13 AM, jolting Daniel from a fitful sleep filled with fragmented dreams.

Dan,

Just finished the pages you sent. Call me IMMEDIATELY. I mean it. Don't make me come over there.

- P

Daniel stared at his phone, momentarily disoriented. He'd sent Patricia the first hundred pages of his manuscript just before midnight, more to prove he was actually writing than to solicit feedback this early in the process. He hadn't expected her to read them overnight, much less respond with such urgency.

Outside, a gray dawn was breaking over Brooklyn, the sky heavy with clouds promising more rain. Daniel's gaze automatically drifted to the windows across the street. Mira's curtains remained drawn, had been for three days now, despite their encounter at the café.

He dialed Patricia's number, bracing himself. She answered on the first ring.

"What the hell, Daniel?" No greeting, just the sharp edge of her voice cutting through the morning quiet.

"Good morning to you too, Pat," he replied, shuffling to the kitchen to start coffee. "I take it you didn't like the pages?"

"Like them? Jesus Christ, Daniel. They're brilliant. Possibly the best thing you've ever written." She paused. "They're also disturbing as hell. I couldn't sleep after reading them."

Daniel felt a surge of pride, followed by unease. "Disturbing how?"

"This character, Lila, she's terrifying because she's so believable. The way you've written her... it's like you're inside the mind of someone genuinely sociopathic." Patricia hesitated. "Where is this coming from, Dan? This doesn't feel like your usual work. It's more... personal somehow."

Daniel watched the coffee drip into his mug, choosing his words carefully. "I've found a new perspective. A way to explore obsession from both sides; the observer and the observed."

"Well, it's working. The publisher is going to eat this up." Another pause. "But I have to ask, this isn't based on anything real, is it? Some of the details feel so specific." The question hung in the air between them. Daniel thought of Mira's amber eyes, the architectural drawings that had scattered across the wet pavement, the way she'd smiled directly at his window as if issuing a challenge.

"It's fiction, Pat," he said finally. "Inspired by observation, maybe, but fiction nonetheless."

"If you say so." She didn't sound entirely convinced. "Send me the next fifty pages when they're ready. And Daniel, be careful with this one. It feels like you're walking a fine line between inspiration and something else."

After hanging up, Daniel carried his coffee to the office and opened his laptop. The manuscript now stood at 112 pages, a miracle of productivity after his prolonged drought. In his fictional world, Marcus and Lila were engaged in an intricate dance of mutual surveillance, each aware of the other's attention but pretending otherwise. The tension was building toward a confrontation that Daniel himself hadn't fully mapped out yet.

He began to type, picking up where he'd left off:

Lila's past was a palimpsest, layers of identities written one over another, each partially visible beneath the current iteration. Marcus had uncovered three so far: the conservatory student who had disappeared after allegations of plagiarism; the gallery assistant in Chicago who had left abruptly following the suspicious death of a wealthy patron; and now the architectural consultant with impeccable credentials that somehow couldn't be verified beyond seven years ago.

What connected these versions of her? What was she building toward with each reinvention? And most importantly, why had she chosen him as her audience?

The words flowed smoothly for nearly two hours before Daniel paused, stretching his tight shoulders. Outside, the promised rain had begun, gentle but persistent. On impulse, he stood and crossed to the window, checking Mira's apartment again. The curtains remained closed.

His phone buzzed with a text message from an unknown number:

Enjoying the view, neighbor? Perhaps we should discuss your next project over dinner. My place, 8 PM tonight. MV

Daniel stared at the message, his pulse quickening. How had she gotten his number? And more disturbingly, how had she known he was at the window just now? He glanced up sharply, scanning her building for any sign of observation. The curtains remained drawn, offering no clues.

He debated how to respond, or whether to respond at all. The invitation felt like stepping willingly into a trap, yet the writer in him couldn't resist the narrative potential of such an encounter. Finally, he typed:

Dinner sounds interesting. Should I bring anything? DM

The response came immediately:

Just your curiosity. And perhaps a copy of your latest work-in-progress. Fair exchange I show you mine, you show me yours.

A chill ran through Daniel. There was no way she could know about his manuscript, about the character he'd based on her. Unless... unless she'd somehow seen it? The thought was impossible, he never printed drafts, and his laptop was password protected.

Yet the specificity of her request left him uneasy. He considered canceling, making an excuse. But the same compulsion that had drawn him to watch her, to transform her into fiction, now pulled him toward this next chapter.

See you at 8. DM

CHAPTER 5: REDEMPTION

At 7:15, Daniel made a decision. He copied selected pages from his manuscript, the ones that described "Lila" but contained nothing about the plot, onto a USB drive. If Mira wanted to see his work, he would show her just enough to gauge her reaction. He would watch her face as she read, searching for signs of recognition, offense, amusement. Whatever game they were playing, he needed more information before his next move.

He then did something he hadn't done in months: he opened the locked bottom drawer of his desk and removed the small leather-bound notebook that contained his research notes from his last published book, The Perfect Victim.

He flipped through the notebook, scanning old interview notes and newspaper clippings. The book was about a professor who manipulated students into elaborate psychological games, eventually driving one to suicide.

Daniel couldn't immediately see a connection to his current situation, to Mira Voss with her architectural drawings and her piano playing. Yet the uneasiness persisted, a whisper at the back of his mind suggesting he was missing something important, something obvious.

He returned the notebook to its drawer, locked it, and pocketed the key. Some instinct told him to be cautious, to keep something in reserve.

At 7:30, Daniel tried calling Patricia once more, but got her voicemail again. He left no message this time, just ended the call and stared at his phone, feeling strangely isolated. In his stories, protagonists often found themselves cut off from support systems just before confronting their antagonist, a narrative device he employed to heighten tension. Now it felt like a cosmic joke at his expense.

He checked his appearance one last time in the hallway mirror; tie or no tie? He removed it, then put it back on, then removed it again, settling finally on the open collar of his shirt as the right balance. He ran a hand through his hair, which had begun to curl slightly as it dried. The effect was less polished than he'd intended, but not entirely unflattering. It softened the sharp angles of his face, which had become more pronounced since the writing drought began.

At 7:45, Daniel stood before his bathroom mirror, examining his reflection critically. He'd shaved, tamed his unruly hair as best he could, and chosen his clothes with unusual care. He looked more put-together than he had in months, the haggard writer transformed into something closer to the author photo on his book jackets.

His hand trembled slightly as he applied cologne, another relic from his book tour days. Was he dressing for a professional meeting, a date, or something else entirely? The uncertainty was both terrifying and exhilarating.

He checked his pockets: keys, phone, wallet, USB drive. All the essentials for a normal dinner, and one unusual item that might prove crucial or completely unnecessary, depending on how the evening unfolded.

On his desk, his laptop glowed with the open manuscript file. After considerable debate, he had decided against bringing any printed pages. The USB drive felt heavy in his pocket, a compromise between caution and curiosity. Whatever game Mira was playing; he wouldn't show his hand so easily.

He took one last look at his apartment before leaving, the neatly arranged books, the vacuumed rugs, the empty coffee mug in the dish drainer. It struck him that he'd prepared as if for a date, despite all his rationalizations about professional curiosity and neighborly gestures.

Some part of him, beyond the writer's obsession with Mira as material, was drawn to her in a more primal way. The stunning eyes, the measured grace of her movements, the enigmatic smile, they had affected him not just as objects of observation, but as forces of attraction.

The realization brought a new dimension of complexity to the evening ahead. He was not just a writer seeking inspiration, not just a man caught in a strange game of mutual surveillance. He was also, simply, a lonely man preparing to dine with a beautiful, mysterious woman. The banality of this truth was almost comforting amid the more unsettling aspects of their connection.

Outside, the night had fully descended, the earlier rain leaving the streets glistening under the streetlights. The air held the sharp scent of wet concrete and fallen leaves, the peculiar melancholy of autumn in the city. Daniel pulled his collar up against a sudden gust of wind as he crossed the street, his gaze inevitably rising to the warm glow of Mira's windows on the third floor.

For a moment, he thought he saw her silhouette framed against the light, watching his approach. But when he blinked, the window was empty, a trick of shadow and reflection, perhaps. Or another move in their strange game.

As he neared Mira's building, he noticed details he couldn't see from his window: the ornate cornices that adorned the roofline, the recently restored façade with its delicate brickwork, the sleek modern security system that seemed at odds with the building's historical character, a steel panel with numbered buttons and an intercom, a small camera lens glinting under the porch light.

The juxtaposition of old and new struck him as significant somehow. Mira preserved historical structures yet installed modern surveillance. She played classical piano but left calculated gaps in her curtains. She presented herself as a chance-met neighbor while orchestrating what felt increasingly like a planned encounter.

He hesitated at the entrance, his writer's imagination conjuring multiple scenarios for what awaited him. In his fictional world, this would be the moment the protagonist should turn back, the warning signs too numerous to ignore. But Daniel had crossed that line days ago, when he first began watching her, transforming her into words on a page without her knowledge or consent.

There was no moral high ground from which to retreat now. Only the path forward, into whatever narrative Mira Voss was constructing around them both. He pressed the buzzer for apartment 3B, directly opposite his own 3A across the street, he realized. Symmetry that felt too perfect to be coincidental.

"Yes?" Her voice through the intercom was distorted but unmistakable, a lower register than he expected, rich with unplaceable accent notes.

"It's Daniel Mercer."

The door buzzed without further comment. Inside, the foyer was elegantly restored, original tile work gleaming beneath modern lighting. A sweeping staircase curved upward; its wooden banister worn smoothly by generations of hands. The building smelled of beeswax polish and something older, a depth of history that newer constructions lacked.

Daniel climbed the stairs to the third floor, each step increasing the strange sense of unreality that had gripped him since receiving her text. The landing was dimly lit, shadows gathering in corners where the light from wall sconces didn't reach. 3A, 3B, 3C—the brass numbers on each door gleamed dully in the low light.

He stood before 3B, raised his hand to knock, when the door opened before his knuckles could touch the wood. Mira stood in the threshold, backlit by the warm glow of her apartment. She wore a simple black dress that accentuated her slender frame, her dark hair loose around her shoulders now instead of in its usual severe bob. The effect was striking, softer than her daytime appearance, but no less controlled.

"Daniel," she said, his name sounding foreign in her mouth, stretched and reshaped by subtle inflections he couldn't quite place. "Right on time. Do come in."

Her apartment was both exactly as he'd observed from his window and somehow completely different up close. The furnishings were minimalist but expensive, the art on the walls abstract and unsettling shapes that suggested human forms in states of distress or transformation. The piano dominated the living room, its glossy surface reflecting the light from designer fixtures above.

"Your home is beautiful," Daniel said, trying to sound casual despite the surreal feeling of stepping into a space he'd only observed from afar. "You've settled in quickly."

"I adapt easily to new environments," Mira replied, gesturing toward the dining area where a table was already set for two. "A necessary skill in my line of work." She moved toward the kitchen. "Wine? I have a lovely Bordeaux breathing."

"Please," Daniel said, following her. Up close, he noticed details that had been invisible from across the street, a small scar near her hairline, the way her left hand occasionally twitched slightly when at rest, the precise, economical quality of her movements.

She poured two glasses of dark red wine, handing one to Daniel. Their fingers brushed briefly, deliberate on her part, he suspected.

"A toast," she suggested, raising her glass. "To new neighbors and... mutual inspiration."

The choice of words sent another wave of unease through Daniel, but he clinked his glass against hers. "To inspiration," he echoed.

Mira's kitchen was state-of-the-art, incongruous with the historical building but perfectly aligned with her aesthetic of controlled precision. She moved confidently through the space, putting final touches on what smelled like coq au vin. Daniel noticed a bookshelf in the adjacent room, filled with volumes on architecture, art history, and his stomach tightened several of his own novels, prominently displayed.

"You're a fan of my work?" he asked, nodding toward the books.

Mira glanced over her shoulder, a small smile playing at her lips.

"I find your psychological insights compelling. Particularly your expertise in creating characters who aren't what they initially seem. Though I've been disappointed by your recent silence. Until now, that is."

The implication hung in the air between them. Daniel sipped his wine, excellent, as she'd promised and decided to test the waters.

"What made you choose this particular building?" he asked. "It's a beautiful restoration, but there must be dozens of similar properties in the area."

Mira began serving the food, her movements graceful and measured. "Let's just say the location offered specific advantages for my current project." She placed a plate before him, the arrangement of food as precise as everything else about her. "I believe in positioning myself optimally for whatever I undertake."

"And what exactly are you undertaking?" Daniel pressed, the writer's curiosity overriding his caution. She seated herself across from him, amber eyes catching the light.

"A comprehensive study. A deep dive into structure and character." Her gaze held his. "Not unlike what you've been doing, I imagine."

Daniel felt exposed, as if she'd somehow read the pages he'd deliberately left behind. "I'm not sure what you mean," he said, taking a bite of the perfectly prepared food to mask his discomfort.

"Come now, Daniel. We can talk without the pretense, can't we? You've been watching me since I arrived. Incorporating me into your new work." She spoke matter-of-factly, without accusation. "I'm not offended. Quite the contrary, I'm flattered to serve as your muse after such a prolonged creative drought."

Daniel nearly choked on his wine. "How could you possibly know about my manuscript?"

Mira's smile deepened, revealing perfect teeth that somehow reminded him of a predator. "Writers observe. So do architects. We both create structures designed to contain and direct human experience." She leaned forward slightly. "The only difference is that I've been aware of our mutual observation from the beginning."

"You've been watching me too," Daniel said, the realization dawning. "But why? I'm nobody special."

"Oh, I wouldn't say that" Mira replied. "Mercer, author of 'The Portrait of Guilt,' 'Beneath Still Waters,' and 'The Perfect Victim' Your work has had... a deep impact on certain lives."

There was something in her tone, a subtle emphasis that raised the hair on Daniel's arms. He thought of his protagonist in the manuscript, discovering connections between his past work and Lila's calculated appearance in his life. "What is this really about, Mira?" he asked quietly. "Why are you here? In that apartment, directly across from mine?"

"Perhaps I simply admire your work and wanted to be close to the creative process," she suggested, but her eyes told a different story. "Or perhaps, like your fictional Lila, I have my own reasons for choosing this particular vantage point."

Daniel stiffened. He hadn't told her about Lila, hadn't mentioned his manuscript at all. "How do you know about that character?"

Mira took a deliberate sip of wine before answering. "The walls between fiction and reality are thinner than most people realize, Daniel. Especially for those who make their living blurring the boundaries." She stood smoothly, collecting their empty plates. "Would you like to see my work now? My own work-in-progress?"

Without waiting for his answer, she walked to the piano and lifted the hinged top to reveal notes, strings and hammers, but a hollow cavity containing a sleek laptop and stacks of precisely organized files. She removed a thick folder and brought it to the table.

"I believe in thorough research," she said, sliding the folder toward him. "It's the foundation of any worthwhile creation."

Daniel opened the folder and felt the blood drain from his face. Inside were photographs of them, of him. Daniel at his desk, visible through his own uncurtained windows. Daniel at the café, long before their "chance" meeting. Daniel went grocery shopping, walking in the park, meeting with Patricia at her midtown office.

And older images too, Daniel at book signings from years ago, at literary festivals, entering his previous apartment building in Manhattan.

"What the hell is this?" he managed, his voice barely audible.

"Context," Mira replied calmly. "Background for my own project." She reached across the table and flipped to the back of the folder, revealing newspaper clippings about a case Daniel had nearly forgotten, a death in Boston five years earlier. The victim's name leapt from the page: Martin Voss, 29, architectural student.

"You're his sister," Daniel whispered, the connections suddenly, horribly clear.

"Yes," Mira confirmed, her composure unwavering. "The sister of the man your book convicted in the public's mind, despite his legal acquittal. The sister of the man who killed himself when he couldn't rebuild his life after your narrative destroyed it."

Daniel remembered the case now, the circumstantial evidence that had pointed to Voss, the trial that had ended in acquittal due to technical errors, the book Daniel had written afterward that had all but named Voss as the killer. He'd never considered the ripple effects of his work beyond book sales and reviews.

"I never claimed—" he began.

"You never used his name directly," Mira interrupted. "A coward's approach, leaving just enough plausible deniability while ensuring everyone knew exactly who you meant." Her voice remained level, which somehow made it more terrifying than if she'd shouted. "Fiction, you would have claimed if he'd sued. Just fiction inspired by real events."

Daniel's mind raced, connecting this revelation to his own manuscript, the story he'd been writing about a woman seeking revenge for her brother's wrongful accusation. Somehow, impossibly, he'd been writing the truth without knowing it.

"What do you want from me?" he asked, acutely aware of how isolated they were, how completely he'd walked into whatever she had planned.

Mira stood and crossed to the kitchen, returning with the wine bottle. She refilled their glasses with steady hands. "Initially? I wanted you to suffer as Martin suffered. To be watched, judged, and ultimately condemned through narrative rather than fact." She took a measured sip. "But then I saw you watching me, and inspiration struck. Something more... fitting."

"What does that mean?" Daniel asked, though he feared he already knew.

"It means, Daniel, that I've been writing too. A psychological thriller about an author who destroys lives with his reckless fictions, only to become trapped in someone else's narrative." She smiled, that same predatory smile. "Life imitating art imitating life, a perfect spiral."

She reached into a drawer beneath the table and removed a manuscript, printed, bound, substantial. The title page read: "The Observer" by Mira Voss. "You should read it," she said, pushing it toward him. "You might find the ending particularly illuminating."

Daniel stared at the manuscript, then back at Mira. In her controlled expression, in the precision of her every movement, he recognized his own fictional creation, except she had existed first. Somehow he had intuited her purpose, had written her motivation without knowing the truth.

"The wine," he said suddenly, looking at his glass. "What did you put in it?"

"Nothing that will harm you permanently," Mira replied. "Just something to help you fully appreciate the final chapters of our story." She checked her watch. "It should be taking effect right about now."

Daniel tried to stand, but his legs felt leaden, unresponsive. The room began to tilt and blur around the edges. Through his dimming vision, he saw Mira rise and move toward him with that same deliberate grace.

"Don't worry," she said, her voice seeming to come from far away. "Unlike you, I've researched my subject thoroughly. I know exactly how this story needs to end." As consciousness slipped away, Daniel's last thought was of his own manuscript, sitting open on his laptop across the street, the scene he'd written just that morning, where Lila finally reveals her true purpose to Marcus over a shared bottle of wine.

Fiction bleeding into reality, or reality that had somehow leaked into his fiction. In his fading awareness, Daniel could no longer tell the difference.

CHAPTER 6: REFLECTIONS

Consciousness returned to Daniel in fragments, disconnected sensations filtering through a haze of confusion. The scratch of fabric against his cheek. A persistent throbbing behind his eyes. The muffled sound of piano music somewhere nearby, each note pristine and deliberate.

He forced his heavy eyelids open, blinking against what seemed like excessive brightness. Gradually, his surroundings sharpened into focus. He was lying on a sofa, Mira's sofa, his wrists bound with what appeared to be zip ties. The elegant restraints matched everything else in her precisely curated life.

The apartment was transformed. Where there had been warm lighting and the intimate setting of their dinner, harsh white utility lamps now stood in strategic corners, illuminating the space with the unforgiving clarity of an operating theater. Or a crime scene.

Mira sat at her piano, back straight, fingers moving across the keys with practiced precision. The piece was something classical that Daniel couldn't identify, complex and unsettling, with discordant notes that seemed deliberately designed to unnerve. She played without sheet music, her eyes closed, as if the composition lived within her muscle memory.

"Bach's Goldberg Variations," she said without turning or missing a note, somehow sensing his consciousness returning. "The Aria. Martin was playing this the night before his suicide." Her fingers continued their measured dance across the keys. "I found him the next morning. Did you know that? I was the one who discovered his body."

Daniel tried to speak, but his mouth felt stuffed with cotton. He worked his jaw, forcing moisture back into his tongue and cheeks.

"Why?" he croaked, then swallowed painfully. "Why are you doing this?"

The music stopped abruptly. Mira turned on the bench, regarding him with clinical interest. "You're a writer, Daniel. You should understand the power of words better than most." She stood and crossed to a sideboard where a pitcher of water waited. Pouring a glass, she approached him, her movements as controlled as ever.

"Careful sips," she instructed, holding the glass to his lips as if he were a child or an invalid. "The sedative causes dehydration."

Daniel drank gratefully despite himself, the cool water reviving him somewhat. His mind raced through possibilities, how long had he been unconscious? Had anyone seen him enter her building? Would Patricia become concerned if he didn't respond to messages?

"You've been out for about three hours," Mira said, again as if reading his thoughts. "No one saw you arrive; I've timed the building's security camera loops quite carefully. And your agent won't miss you until tomorrow at the earliest, given your history of ignoring her calls." She set the water glass down with a precise click against the coffee table. "I've considered all the variables, Daniel. That's what I do."

"What exactly do you plan to do with me?" he asked, struggling to maintain composure as fear chilled his blood.

"I told you before, I will create a fitting ending." Mira returned to the piano bench, this time facing him. "But I'm not a monster, despite what you might think. I'm not going to physically harm you in any significant way." Her amber eyes gleamed in the harsh light. "That would be... inelegant. And far too quick."

She reached beside the bench and lifted her manuscript; the thick stack of pages that had been the last thing Daniel saw before losing consciousness. "Have you ever wondered what it's like to be a character rather than an author? To have your actions, your fate, determined by someone else's imagination?"

"Mira," Daniel said, trying to sound reasonable despite his terror, "I understand you're angry about your brother. But I didn't kill him. I wrote a book based on publicly available information. I never claimed it was anything but fiction."

"Fiction," she repeated, the word sharp as glass between her teeth. "Such a convenient shield for cowards." She opened the manuscript, finding a marked page. "Let me read you something from my own work of 'fiction,' Daniel."

She began to read in a clear, measured voice:

"'The author had never considered the consequences of his words beyond sales figures and critical acclaim. Each character he falsely labeled as 'fictional' had left wreckage in the real world. There were lives derailed, reputations destroyed, psychological damage that couldn't be undone with a simple disclaimer. He had wielded his talent like a weapon without accepting responsibility for the carnage.'"

Mira looked up from the page. "Sound familiar? It should. It's essentially what you've been writing about me in your manuscript, a woman seeking justice for her brother, destroyed by false narrative. The key difference is that my version has the benefit of being true."

Daniel strained against his restraints, plastic cutting into his wrists. "How do you know what I've been writing? Have you been in my apartment?"

A slight smile curved her lips. "I haven't needed to be. Not physically." She set aside her manuscript and retrieved a tablet from the piano bench. Tapping the screen, she turned it toward Daniel.

On the display was his own manuscript, the exact file that should have been open only on his password-protected laptop across the street.

"Remote access isn't particularly difficult if you have the right skills," Mira explained, scrolling through his pages. "I've been reading along since day three of your renewed creativity. Quite the coincidence, isn't it? How accurately you've captured my motivations while allegedly knowing nothing about me?"

Daniel's mind reeled. She'd been reading his work all along, watching him create a fictional version of exactly what was happening now. The violation felt intimate, invasive in a way that went beyond the physical danger of his current situation.

"What happens now?" he asked, focusing on keeping his voice steady.

Mira set the tablet aside and stood, moving to the window, the same window he'd watched her through for weeks. She drew back the curtain, revealing his apartment across the street, his own office window clearly visible, lights still on from when he'd left earlier.

"Now we progress to the next phase," she said. "You see, Daniel, I've been constructing this narrative carefully, building a case, collecting evidence, creating a pattern that will be unmistakable when it's discovered."

She turned back to him, her expression almost regretful. "Your recent search history is particularly troubling, all those queries about stalking laws, about researching someone without their knowledge. Your manuscript itself reads like the confession of a man obsessed, incorporating increasingly accurate details about a woman he watches compulsively from his window."

Cold realization washed over Daniel. "You're framing me."

"'Framing' suggests fabrication," Mira corrected. "I'm merely highlighting what's already there, your voyeurism, your inappropriate fixation, your transformation of a real person into a character for your commercial benefit." She returned to where he lay bound. "You've been writing our story all along, Daniel. I'm simply ensuring it reaches the proper audience."

She retrieved a small case from beneath the coffee table and opened it, revealing a hypodermic needle.

"What is that?" Daniel asked, unable to keep the panic from his voice.

"Another sedative," Mira replied calmly. "Milder than the first. You'll remain semiconscious but compliant. Necessary for the next scene in our narrative."

"Please," Daniel said, desperation overtaking pride. "Whatever Martin suffered, this won't undo it. This won't bring him back."

Something flickered in Mira's amber eyes, a momentary crack in her perfect composure. "No, it won't bring him back. Nothing will. But it will balance the scales." She prepared the injection with practiced movements. "Martin lost everything because of the story you told. His reputation, his career prospects, eventually his will to live. Now you'll understand what that's like, to be trapped with no way to rewrite the ending."

Before Daniel could respond, she administered the injection with swift precision. Unlike the wine's slow-building sedation, this drug worked almost instantly. He remained conscious but felt his muscles relaxing involuntarily, his thoughts becoming detached from his physical form.

"Good," Mira murmured, checking his pupils. "Now we can proceed." Through a dreamlike haze, Daniel experienced what followed as a series of disconnected scenes, like fragments of a film spliced together without transitions:

Mira cutting the zip ties, guiding his unresisting body to stand... The sensation of his own clothing being arranged carefully, her clinical touch straightening his collar, positioning his arms... The click of a camera from multiple angles... Her voice, speaking softly as she worked, words he couldn't quite grasp but that seemed to be directions, instructions to his unresponsive body... The peculiar feeling of watching himself perform actions he hadn't chosen, as if he were both a puppet and a reluctant audience.

Later, he couldn't tell how much later, he was seated at her dining table again, a pen in his limp hand. Mira stood behind him, her breath warm against his ear as she guided his fingers across paper. "Your handwriting is quite distinctive, Daniel," she murmured. "Those years of signing books has made your signature particularly consistent. Helpful for our purposes."

She guided his hand, forming words he couldn't focus on clearly. Multiple pages, his drugged hand following her direction. Through the haze, Daniel understood she was creating evidence, notes in his handwriting, perhaps a confession or documentation of obsession. His mind rebelled, but his body complied, betrayed by whatever compound now flowed through his system.

"Almost done," Mira said eventually, her voice reaching him as if through water. "Just the final scene to stage."

More fragmented impressions followed: The sensation of being moved again... Cold night air suddenly against his face... The familiar smells of his own apartment... Mira's efficient movements as she positioned him in his office chair, arranged his hands on his keyboard... The glow of his laptop screen, his manuscript open just as he'd left it hours earlier.

"I've added a final chapter to your story, Daniel," she said, her voice seeming to come from far away though she stood directly behind him. "I think you'll find it fitting. art completing life." Her cool fingers brushed his cheek in an almost tender gesture. "I've enjoyed our collaboration."

Time slipped away again. When awareness next solidified, Daniel was alone in his apartment, slumped in his desk chair, dawn light filtering through his windows. Across the street, Mira's curtains were open, her apartment appearing empty and undisturbed, as if the events of the night had been nothing but a vivid nightmare.

But the lingering heaviness in his limbs, the dull ache where the needle had punctured his skin, and his rumpled clothes from the previous evening confirmed the reality of his experience. Daniel forced his still-sluggish body to move, checking himself for injuries. Beyond the injection site and faint marks on his wrists from the zip ties, he appeared physically unharmed.

His laptop sat open before him. With trembling fingers, he scrolled through his manuscript, finding a new section added at the end, words he hadn't written but that appeared seamlessly integrated with his own work:

The obsession had consumed Marcus entirely, blinding him to the danger until it was too late. As Lila's plan reached its conclusion, he realized the terrible symmetry of their situation: he had destroyed her brother through narrative, and now she would destroy him the same way. The evidence she had carefully arranged. his notes, his photographs, his increasingly unhinged manuscript, would tell a story he would be powerless to rewrite. And as with all compelling fiction, it contained just enough truth to be believable.

When they found him, the authorities would see only what Lila had crafted for them to see: the portrait of a writer whose fixation on his subject had crossed from professional interest into dangerous obsession. The boundary between author and character, between creator and creation, had dissolved completely.

In his final lucid moment, Marcus understood with perfect clarity: he had not written this story. It had been writing him all along.

Daniel stared at the words, his blood running cold. This wasn't just Mira taunting him; it was a blueprint, a warning of what was coming next.

With shaking hands, he reached for his phone to call Patricia, then hesitated. What would he tell her? That his neighbor had drugged him and was framing him as a stalker? That somehow she had been reading his manuscript remotely while he wrote it. That the character he'd created was actually based on a real woman whose brother had killed himself because of one of his books?

The story sounded delusional even to his own ears. And Mira would have anticipated this move, would have prepared for it, would have ensured that any attempt to expose her would only make him appear more unbalanced. He looked across the street again. Mira's apartment remained still and empty. Was she watching him somehow, even now? Waiting for his next move in their twisted game?

Daniel turned back to his laptop, scrolling frantically through his browser history. Just as she'd claimed, it contained multiple searches about stalking, surveillance techniques, and privacy laws, searches he had no memory of making. Planted while he was drugged, or remotely inserted into his computer?

A notification pinged on his screen, an email from Patricia:

Dan,

Just got a disturbing call from a woman named Mira Voss who says she's your neighbor. Claims you've been watching her, taking photos, leaving notes. Says she's concerned and wanted to reach out to someone who knows you before going to the authorities. What the hell is going on? Call me IMMEDIATELY.

- P

The trap was closing around him, exactly as Mira had written it would. Daniel glanced at his phone, should he call Patricia? Try to explain? But explaining would mean admitting to the observation that had started all this, the manuscript based on a woman he'd watched without her knowledge.

As the drug's effects continued to fade, Daniel's mind raced through scenarios, searching for a way out of the narrative Mira had constructed. But each potential path seemed to lead back to the same conclusion she had already written for him.

Across the street, a curtain moved slightly. Mira stood at her window now, watching him openly, a mug of coffee in her hand. When their eyes met, she raised the mug in a small toast, her expression calm and satisfied. She had the look of an author who knows exactly how her story will end.

CHAPTER 6: COUNTERMOVES

Daniel pulled the blinds closed with a sharp snap, cutting off Mira's smug gaze from across the street. His hands trembled, from the lingering effects of the drugs, from fear, from rage, he couldn't tell which dominated. Pacing the confines of his office, he forced himself to think like the writer he was, to analyze the narrative structure Mira had constructed around him.

In his thrillers, this would be the moment when the protagonist either surrendered to inevitable fate or found the single overlooked flaw in the antagonist's perfect plan. But real life rarely offered such clean literary solutions.

His phone buzzed again, Patricia, now calling rather than just emailing. Daniel silenced it. Whatever he told her now would only sound defensive or delusional. Mira had outmaneuvered him, making the first move by contacting his agent directly. A preemptive strike that transformed any explanation he might offer into the fabrications of a man caught in inappropriate behavior.

Daniel returned to his laptop, scanning through his files. If Mira had remote access to his computer, he couldn't trust anything on it. He needed to assume she could see everything he did, read every word he wrote, monitor his searches and communications.

"Think," he muttered, pressing his palms against his temples. "What would one of your characters do?"

His gaze fell on the manuscript, the story that had begun as fiction and somehow morphed into prophetic reality. In the narrative he'd created, Lila's elaborate revenge hinged on Marcus remaining passive, reacting rather than acting. The symmetry struck him now: Mira expected him to behave like a character, not an author.

Daniel reached for a legal pad and pen, analog, unhackable. He began listing what he knew for certain:

Mira Voss is Martin Voss's sister.

Martin committed suicide after Daniel's book implicated him in a murder.

Mira has been planning this for months, possibly years.

She has remote access to his computer.

She has created evidence framing him as obsessed with her.

She's contacted Patricia to establish her concerns about his behavior.

No physical evidence of his drugging likely remains in his system by now.

The facts, laid bare, presented a grim picture. He flipped the page and wrote: OPTIONS?

The most obvious solution, going to the police would almost certainly backfire. Without evidence beyond his word, his story would sound paranoid and self-serving. Worse, it would give Mira exactly what she wanted: public acknowledgment of his "fixation" on her.

Patricia might believe him, but without proof, what could she do? The same problem applied to friends, family, anyone he might turn to for help. Mira had constructed her trap too carefully, ensuring any attempt to escape would only ensnare him further.

A new thought struck him suddenly. If Mira could access his computer remotely, the connection worked both ways. In theory, he could trace it back, find evidence of her intrusion. Daniel had limited technical skills, but he knew people who didn't.

He retrieved his old phone from a desk drawer, a backup device he kept charged but rarely used. If Mira had compromised his primary phone, she might not know about this one. He powered it on and texted Reza, a former IT specialist he'd consulted for technical details in his second novel:

Need urgent cybersecurity help. Possible computer breach. Can you come to my place today? Emergency. Will pay whatever rate.

While waiting for a response, Daniel continued analyzing his situation. Mira's plan depended on specific evidence, the searches on his computer, the manuscript itself, whatever notes and photos she'd fabricated. If he could somehow discredit or destroy that evidence...

His old phone buzzed with Reza's reply:

Serious timing. I'm in BK for a conference. Can be there in 1 hr. Still at the same place?

Daniel responded with his address, feeling the first flicker of hope since waking from his drugged state. He spent the next hour meticulously checking his apartment for anything Mira might have planted during her visit. He found nothing obvious, but the search gave him purpose, and kept the panic at bay.

When Reza arrived, a compact man with perpetually disheveled hair and sharp, observant eyes, Daniel offered only a partial explanation: he suspected someone had hacked his computer and was accessing his files, possibly for literary theft. Reza raised an eyebrow but didn't press for details. "Let's see what we're dealing with," he said, settling at Daniel's desk and opening a laptop of his own. "Don't touch your computer while I work."

For the next two hours, Daniel watched Reza run diagnostics and security scans, occasionally muttering in Farsi when he discovered something interesting. Finally, he leaned back in the chair.

"You were right," he said. "Someone installed a fairly sophisticated remote access trojan on your system. Been there for about three weeks, based on the timestamps." He pointed to lines of code on his screen. "They've had complete access, files, camera, microphone, the works."

Daniel's stomach clenched. "Can you tell who did it?"

"Not definitively, but they're connecting from an IP address very close by." Reza glanced toward the window with the closed blinds. "Like, really close by. Across the street close by."

"Can you block them? Remove their access?"

Reza nodded. "Already did. Purged the RAT, updated your security, changed all relevant access codes." He hesitated. "But Daniel, if this person is physically nearby, they could just install another one if they get access to your computer again."

"Could you..." Daniel chose his words carefully. "Could you do the same to them? Access their system?"

Reza's expression turned cautious.

"Ah....That would be illegal. Just removing malware from your own system is self-defense. Hacking someone else's is a federal crime."

"Even if they hacked me first?"

"Two wrongs, man." Reza shook his head. "But I can set up monitoring that will alert you if they try to access your system again, and secure your computer against physical tampering." He gave Daniel a searching look. "Want to tell me what's really going on? This doesn't feel like a simple literary theft."

Daniel considered how much to reveal. Reza was trustworthy, but involving him further could put him at risk. "It's complicated," he said finally. "Let's just say I'm dealing with someone who has a personal vendetta."

Reza didn't look satisfied with the explanation but nodded anyway. "Whatever you're mixed up in, be careful. This wasn't amateur hour, whoever did this knows what they're doing."

After Reza left, having fortified Daniel's digital defenses as much as possible, Daniel returned to the window and carefully peered through a gap in the blinds. Mira's apartment appeared empty; curtains open again as if inviting his observation. A power move, he realized, showing she had nothing to hide while he literally kept himself in darkness.

His phone, his regular phone, buzzed with another call from Patricia. He couldn't avoid her forever. Taking a deep breath, he answered. "Daniel, what the hell is going on?" Patricia's voice was tight with concern. "This woman called me again; said she's found notes you've left in her mailbox. She's talking about a restraining order."

"Notes? That's impossible," Daniel said, his voice hoarse. "Pat, I need you to listen carefully. This woman, Mira Voss, she's Martin Voss's sister."

A beat of silence. "Martin Voss? From the Boston case? The one who...."

"Killed himself after my book came out. Yes." Daniel paced the length of his office. "She blames me for his death. She's been planning some kind of revenge."

"Daniel..." Patricia's tone shifted to something like cautious concern. "I looked her up after she called. She's a respected architectural consultant. No criminal record, excellent professional reputation."

"Of course she is," Daniel said, frustration mounting. "She's methodical. She's spent years crafting a perfect image while planning this."

"Planning what exactly? What are you saying she's done?"

Daniel hesitated. How could he explain that she'd drugged him, manipulated him, created false evidence, all without a single witness or piece of proof? Put into words, his claims sounded exactly like the desperate deflections of a man caught in inappropriate behavior.

"She's framing me," he said finally. "Making it look like I've been stalking her, obsessing over her."

The silence that followed was damning. "Daniel," Patricia said carefully, "I need to ask you directly: have you been watching this woman? Has she become some kind of... fixation for you?"

"I observed her," Daniel admitted, knowing how it sounded. "For the book. My new protagonist is based partly on her. But it wasn't—it isn't what she's making it out to be."

Another weighted silence. "Your manuscript... the pages you sent me. The character Lila; that's based on her?"

"Yes, but..."

"Jesus, Daniel. Do you realize how this looks? The detailed descriptions of her daily routines, her appearance it reads like surveillance notes." Patricia's voice had taken on a professional distance that frightened him more than anger would have. "And now you're claiming she's some mastermind out for revenge because of a book you wrote years ago?"

"I know how it sounds," Daniel said desperately. "But she drugged me last night. She's been accessing my computer remotely. I just had an IT specialist confirm it."

"Do you have proof of any of this? The drugging? Anything concrete?"

Daniel closed his eyes. "No."

"Then I strongly suggest you stop all contact with this woman immediately. Don't look at her apartment, don't write about her, don't even think about her if you can help it." Patricia's voice softened slightly. "You've been under immense pressure with this book. Maybe the stress, the isolation"

"I'm not having a breakdown, Pat," Daniel interrupted, anger flaring. "She orchestrated all of this. She moved across from me deliberately. She's been playing a game from the beginning."

"Alright," Patricia said, clearly unconvinced. "Either way, my advice stands. Stay away from her. I'm over tomorrow. We need to talk about this in person."

After ending the call, Daniel slumped against the wall. Patricia, his most reliable ally, already half-believed Mira's version of events. If he couldn't convince his own agent of the truth, what chance did he have with anyone else?

His gaze fell on his manuscript, the story that had begun as fiction but now seemed prophetically, impossibly entwined with reality. An idea formed, desperate but potentially effective. If Mira had used his writing against him, perhaps he could use it to save himself.

Daniel returned to his desk and opened a new document, separate from his compromised manuscript. He began to type rapidly, creating not fiction but a detailed chronology: his first observation of Mira, the development of his character based on her, their meeting at the café, the dinner invitation, everything that had happened in her apartment, including the drugging and manipulation. He included every detail he could remember, focusing on facts rather than emotions or interpretations.

When finished, he transferred the document to a USB drive, then deleted it from his computer. If Mira still had some means of access despite Reza's security measures, she wouldn't see this direct counterattack.

Next, he began a new narrative, a fictional story about a woman who methodically frames her neighbor for stalking as revenge for a perceived wrong. He described her methods in detail: the remote computer access, the fabricated evidence, the careful cultivation of witnesses like Patricia. The story presented as fiction what he believed to be happening in reality, laid out with the psychological insight that had made his thrillers successful.

This, he left on his computer, a challenge, a signal to Mira that he understood her game and was prepared to play it differently. If she was still monitoring his activities, she would see it soon enough. As evening fell, Daniel ordered food delivery, careful to use his old phone for the call. When the delivery person arrived, Daniel casually asked if they'd made any other deliveries to the building across the street.

"Yeah, actually," the young woman said. "To 3B, right before yours. Lady tipped really well."

"Did she seem...okay?" Daniel asked, trying to sound merely neighborly. "I saw some commotion over there earlier."

The delivery person shrugged. "Seemed fine. Said she was packing for a trip, though. Bunch of suitcases by the door."

Daniel's pulse quickened. "A trip? Did she say where?"

"Nah, just that she was heading out tonight." The delivery person eyed him curiously. "You two friends or something?"

"Acquaintances," Daniel said, forcing a casual tone. "Thanks for letting me know."

After closing the door, Daniel rushed to the window. Through the gap in the blinds, he could see lights on in Mira's apartment and movement suggesting packing activity. Was she really leaving? Or was this another element of her performance, designed to make him panic or act impulsively?

If she left, what would she leave behind? All the fabricated evidence pointing to his obsession, perfectly positioned for discovery. Would she file a report before leaving, ensuring authorities would find exactly what she wanted them to find?

Daniel checked the time: 7:42 PM. Whatever Mira planned to do; he needed to act first. Filing a police report himself seemed futile without evidence, but there might be another approach, confrontation, recorded on his terms.

He retrieved his digital voice recorder a tool he often used for capturing ideas when writing and tested it. Then, checking that his old phone was fully charged, he slipped both devices into his pocket and headed for the door.

Across the darkening street, Mira's windows glowed with warm light, revealing glimpses of her moving efficiently through her apartment. From this distance, she looked so ordinary, so harmless. Only Daniel knew the calculating mind behind that carefully composed exterior.

As he stepped outside into the cool October evening, Daniel felt a strange calm settle over him. In his books, this would be the climactic confrontation, protagonist and antagonist finally facing each other with truth as the only weapon. Fiction had blurred with reality once already in this twisted narrative.

Perhaps it was time to write a different ending than the one Mira had planned.

CHAPTER 7: CONFRONTATION

Daniel crossed the street with purpose, each step carrying him closer to confrontation. The evening air felt electric against his skin, as if the atmosphere itself recognized the stakes of what he was about to do. He checked his recorder once more, ensuring it was capturing.

The building's entrance required a key fob, but luck was on his side. A young couple exited just as he approached, and he caught the door before it closed, nodding in thanks as he slipped inside. The lobby was modest but well-maintained, potted plants flanking a row of mailboxes. Daniel located 3B on the directory and headed for the elevator.

His heart hammered against his ribs as he ascended. Was he walking into another trap? Probably. But this time he was clearheaded, armed with awareness and the truth. The elevator doors slid open on the third floor, and Daniel paused, taking a deep breath before proceeding down the carpeted hallway.

Outside 3B, he hesitated only briefly before knocking. Three sharp raps that seemed to echo his heartbeat. For several seconds, nothing. Then footsteps approached from within. The door opened, and there stood Mira, dressed in dark jeans and a cream-colored blouse, her expression shifting instantly from neutral to surprise to controlled amusement.

"Daniel," she said, leaning against the doorframe. "This is unexpected."

"Is it?" Daniel kept his voice level, aware of the recorder in his pocket. "I heard you're leaving town."

Mira's smile didn't reach her eyes. "News travels fast in this neighborhood. Yes, I have an early flight tomorrow. Professional commitment."

"Convenient timing."

"She tilted her head slightly. "I'm not sure what you mean."

"May I come in?" Daniel asked. "Or would you prefer we have this conversation in the hallway?"

Mira studied him for a moment, calculation evident behind her gaze. Then she stepped back, opening the door wider. "By all means."

The apartment was indeed in a state of organized chaos, Daniel could see suitcases open on the floor, clothes laid out across the sofa, toiletries arranged neatly on the coffee table. Everything perfectly consistent with her story, Daniel noted. She'd always been thorough.

"I assume you're here about the conversation I had with your agent," Mira said, crossing to the kitchen where a half-empty glass of wine sat beside an open bottle. "Would you like some? It's a decent Shiraz."

"No, thank you," Daniel replied, remembering all too well what had happened the last time she offered him a drink. "I'm here because we both know what you're doing."

"And what am I doing, Daniel?"

She took a deliberate sip of wine, watching him over the rim of her glass.

"Executing a calculated revenge plan." He remained standing, positioning himself where he could see most of the apartment. "Martin's suicide hit you hard. You needed someone to blame."

Something flickered across Mira's features, a momentary crack in her composure. "My brother was broken by your book. Your 'creative interpretation' of events destroyed him."

"I wrote about a case that was already public record."

"You wrote speculation disguised as insight!" Her voice sharpened, then immediately recalled to controlled calm. "But that's not why you're here, is it? You believe I'm... what? Framing you for harassment?"

Daniel maintained eye contact. "I know you are. The remote access to my computer, the fabricated evidence, contacting Patricia, it's all part of a narrative you've constructed."

Mira laughed; the sound genuine enough to be unsettling. "This is exactly what Patricia was concerned about. You've developed a paranoid fixation, Daniel. First observing me for your book, now concocting elaborate conspiracy theories." She set down her wine glass. "It would be sad if it weren't so concerning."

"I had my system checked," Daniel countered. "The remote access was confirmed by an IT specialist this afternoon."

"Remote access?" Mira's eyebrows rose. "Daniel, I'm an architectural consultant, not a hacker. Whatever you found on your computer has nothing to do with me."

She moved toward one of the suitcases, casually rearranging its contents. "Look, I understand creative people can develop intense fixations. The line between research and obsession can blur. That's why I reached out to your agent rather than the police, I thought she might help you get perspective."

"After you drugged me," Daniel said flatly.

Mira stopped, turning to face him with a perfect expression of bewildered concern. "Drugged you? Daniel, we had dinner. You had several glasses of wine. If you experienced some adverse reaction...."

"You put something in my drink." "This is exactly what I'm talking about."

She shook her head sadly. "These delusions, they're troubling. Have you spoken to someone professional about these thoughts?"

Daniel felt a surge of frustration. The conversation was following precisely the script she'd prepared, his accusations sounding increasingly unhinged against her reasonable denials. He needed to change tactics.

"Tell me about the book Martin wrote," he said suddenly. Mira paused, genuine surprise crossing her face before she could mask it.

"What?"

"Your brother's unpublished manuscript," Daniel continued, building on the momentary advantage of having caught her off-guard. "The one he was working on before his death. You have it, don't you?" This was a complete shot in the dark, based on nothing but instinct and storytelling logic. If Martin had been a writer like his sister claimed, there might have been a manuscript. And if there was, Mira might have it; might even consider it precious.

The slight widening of her eyes told him his random arrow had somehow hit a target.

"I don't know what you're talking about," she said, but her voice had lost its practiced smoothness.

"I think you do," Daniel pressed forward. "I think Martin was writing something important, something that might change how people saw him, how they saw the case. And I think that manuscript might tell a different story than the one you've been telling."

Mira's composure slipped further. "You don't know anything about Martin or his work."

"Maybe not," Daniel acknowledged. "But I know stories, Mira. I know when someone is crafting a story, controlling how information unfolds. Just like you've been doing with me." He took a calculated risk, moving toward her bookshelf where several leather-bound journals were arranged. "Is it here? Among his journals, perhaps?"

"Don't touch those!" The sharpness in her voice confirmed he'd struck another nerve.

Daniel reached for one of the journals. "What's in here that you don't want me to see, Mira?"

She moved quickly, placing herself between him and the bookshelf. "You need to leave. Now."

"Why?" Daniel held his ground. "What are you afraid I'll find? The truth about Martin? About you?" "The truth?" Something darkened in Mira's expression.

"You wouldn't recognize the truth if it was handed to you on one of your pretentious manuscript pages."

"Try me," Daniel challenged her.

For a long moment, they stood in tense silence, the air between them charged with unspoken hostility. Then Mira's shoulders relaxed slightly, a different calculation settling in her eyes. "Fine," she said, her voice softening to something almost intimate. "You want the truth, Daniel? The truth is you're right about one thing; I did plan this. Moving across from you wasn't a coincidence."

Daniel felt a rush of vindication, quickly tempered by wariness. This admission came too easily. "But it's not what you think," she continued. "I needed to understand the man who wrote about my brother, who he really was, not just the public persona."

She moved to a desk in the corner, opened a drawer, and removed a thin file. "Here's your 'evidence.' Notes I've taken since moving here. Observations of your habits, your visitors, your writing schedule. Call it research if you like."

Daniel didn't move to take the file. "Why? What were you hoping to find?"

"Insight," Mira said simply. "Into how someone could write so convincingly about another person's inner thoughts, their motivations, their breaking points, and get it so wrong."

She returned the file to the drawer. "Martin wasn't what your book painted him to be. He wasn't a calculating manipulator who orchestrated a perfect crime and then cracked under scrutiny. He was a sensitive, troubled man who got caught in circumstances beyond his control."

"The evidence..."

"Was circumstantial at best," she interrupted. "You filled in the gaps with your imagination and presented it as truth. You made him a monster for the sake of your story."

Daniel processed this, trying to determine where truth ended and manipulation began. "And drugging me? Was that also for 'research'?"

Something shifted in Mira's expression again, a minute tell that would have been imperceptible if he hadn't been watching so carefully. "I never drugged you, Daniel. That's your paranoia speaking." She returned to her packing, the dismissal clear in her posture.

"But I am taking our conversation to the police before I leave town. Your behavior has escalated beyond what I'm comfortable managing privately."

"They'll find it interesting that you admitted to moving across from me deliberately, to studying me," Daniel countered. "That you kept files on me."

Mira smiled thinly. "What I've done is research for a memoir about my brother's life and death including the impact of your book. What you've done is fixate on your neighbor to an unhealthy degree, then concoct an elaborate conspiracy theory when confronted about it."

She closed one suitcase with a decisive zip. "Now, I have an early flight. Unless you'd like me to call the police right now instead of tomorrow, I suggest you leave."

Daniel stood his ground. "The remote access to my computer was real. Someone has been monitoring everything I do, reading my files, watching through my webcam. If it wasn't you, who was it?"

For the briefest moment, something like uncertainty crossed Mira's face. It was subtle, a slight hesitation, a flicker of genuine question, but Daniel caught it. "That's not my concern," she said finally. "Perhaps you should consider that your paranoia might have more than one target."

"Or perhaps," came a new voice from the apartment's entryway, "you both should consider that you're not the only players in this game."

Daniel and Mira both turned, startled. A man stood in the open doorway, lean, with silver-streaked dark hair and the kind of face that seemed permanently amused by a private joke. He held a small device in one hand, pointed toward them.

"Martin?" Mira whispered, her face draining of color.

The man's smile widened. "Not quite. Though I appreciate the family resemblance is strong."

Daniel's mind raced, processing implications. "You're..."

"Michael Voss," the man supplied smoothly. "The other brother. The one neither of you bothered to mention in your little drama." He stepped fully into the apartment, closing the door behind him. "And I've been finding your performances absolutely fascinating."

Both Daniel and Mira stood frozen, the tension in the room shifting like quicksand beneath their feet. "You were dead," Mira finally said, her voice barely above a whisper. "You died in that boating accident. Five years ago."

Michael's smile remained fixed as he moved further into the apartment, the small device which Daniel now recognized as a signal jammer, still held casually in his palm. "Reports of my death were, as they say, greatly exaggerated. A necessary disappearance, orchestrated with the help of our tragically deceased brother."

Daniel's mind raced to catch up. "Martin helped you fake your death.

“Martin was always the loyal one," Michael replied, settling into an armchair as if he'd been invited. "Too loyal, perhaps. It became his undoing."

Mira had gone completely still, her face a mask of conflicting emotions. "Why?" she asked, the single word loaded with years of grief and betrayal. "Why would you do that to us? To Mom? She never recovered from losing you."

"Necessity, dear sister." Michael's casual tone carried an undercurrent of steel. "When certain investments go catastrophically wrong and certain people with certain connections start asking pointed questions, disappearing becomes an attractive option."

He glanced at Daniel with unexpected appreciation. "Your book actually did me an enormous favor. All that attention on Martin, the police, the media, the true crime enthusiasts, it ensured no one was looking in my direction."

Daniel felt sickened. "Martin's suicide... was it because of my book, or because of you?"

"A complicated question," Michael mused. "Martin was always fragile, brilliant but burdened by conscience. Helping me disappear weighed on him, especially as the investigations intensified. Your book didn't help, certainly. But the final straw was my request that he sign over his portion of our inheritance to offshore accounts I could access."

"You bastard," Mira whispered, composure cracking into raw fury. "He worshipped you, and you used him until he broke."

Michael's expression hardened momentarily. "I loved Martin. But he understood sacrifice, family above all." He turned his attention back to Daniel. "As for you, Mr. Mercer, I've been monitoring your activities with great interest ever since my sister decided to insert herself into your life."

Daniel's suspicions crystallized. "You're the one who hacked my computer."

"Guilty as charged," Michael acknowledged with a slight nod. "Initially just to keep tabs on my sister's revenge project. I was curious how far she'd take it." His smile turned appreciative. "You play a long game, Mira. I've always admired that about you."

Mira's face had returned to its controlled mask, but Daniel could see the calculation behind her eye reevaluating, adjusting to this new reality.

"What do you want?" she asked flatly.

"Many things," Michael replied. "But at the moment, I'd like Mr. Mercer here to understand his role in our family drama."

He turned to Daniel. "You see, when Mira started her little project, moving across from you, studying you, planning to destroy your reputation as you supposedly destroyed Martin's, I recognized an opportunity. You're a man with substantial resources, an established name. Useful."

"Useful for what?" Daniel asked, the recorder still running in his pocket, capturing this impossible conversation.

"Leverage," Michael said simply. "Mira intended to frame you as an obsessive stalker. I decided to enhance her efforts, add some truly concerning search histories to your browser, some encrypted files that would raise serious flags if discovered by authorities."

Daniel felt cold dread spreading through him. "What kind of files?"

"Nothing you want found on your devices, believe me," Michael replied with a casual menace. "The kind that can't be explained away as research for a novel."

Mira stepped forward, her shock giving way to focused anger. "Whatever game you're playing, Michael, leave Daniel out of it. This was between him and me."

Michael laughed, the sound genuine and somehow more disturbing for it. "How protective you've become of your target. Interesting."

He turned back to Daniel. "Here's the situation, Mr. Mercer. Those files remain on a hidden partition of your computer, undetectable by your friend Reza but easily accessible to me. Whether they stay hidden or find their way to law enforcement depends entirely on your cooperation."

"With what?" Daniel demanded.

"A simple financial arrangement," Michael explained. "Your next advance is quite substantial, I understand. Two million for a three-book deal. I'll need most of that. Let's say seventy-five percent."

"You're blackmailing me," Daniel said flatly.

Michael shrugged. "I prefer to think of it as compensation for the pain your work caused my family. Poetic justice."

Daniel glanced at Mira, who stood rigid with tension, her face unreadable. "And what's her role in this revised plan?"

"Mira has her own choice to make," Michael said, his tone hardening as he addressed his sister. "Family loyalty or... whatever this is you've developed for the man you were planning to destroy."

Mira's jaw tightened. "You abandoned us, let us believe you were dead, drove Martin to suicide, and now you talk about family loyalty?"

"I did what was necessary to survive," Michael countered. "As I always have. As our father taught us." He leaned forward, his casual manner dropping away to reveal something colder. "The question is whether you remember those lessons, sister."

The room fell into tense silence, the three of them locked in a triangle of conflicting interests. Daniel's mind raced through options, each seeming more impossible than the last. The recorder in his pocket captured everything, but would it matter? Would anyone believe this twisted story?

Mira moved first, crossing to the kitchen with measured steps. "I need a drink for this conversation." She reached for her wine glass, then paused. "Daniel? Michael? Last offer."

Michael smiled. "Why not? A family reunion deserves a toast, doesn't it?"

"Nothing for me," Daniel said automatically, still processing the situation.

Mira poured a second glass for Michael, her movements deliberate and controlled. She handed it to him with a smile that didn't reach her eyes. "To family," she said, raising her own glass.

Michael took the wine, his expression softening momentarily. "You always did have excellent taste, little sister." He raised the glass in a salute before taking a deep sip.

Daniel watched the exchange with growing unease. Something in Mira's posture, in the calculated way she'd offered the wine...

"Now," Michael continued, setting his glass down. "Let's discuss the practical arrangements of our new partnership."

Mira returned to her position near the suitcases; her expression unreadable. "Before we do that, I have a question." She pulled her phone from her pocket. "How did you access Daniel's computer? What method?"

Michael raised an eyebrow at the question. "Why does that matter now?"

"Professional curiosity," Mira replied. "If I'm going to be part of this, I want to understand exactly what we're dealing with."

Michael studied her for a moment before answering. "A customized trojan delivered via an email attachment. Supposedly from his publisher, containing revised contract details. Basic but effective."

Mira nodded, then turned to Daniel. "And you never suspected an email from Patricia?"

"It looked completely legitimate," Daniel said, understanding dawning. "The document even had the correct letterhead, contract numbers..."

"Because I had access to the real ones," Michael explained with a hint of pride. "Mira's not the only one who can do thorough research."

Mira smiled thinly, typing something on her phone. "You always were meticulous, Michael. It's how I knew it was you."

Michael's expression shifted, wariness replacing confidence.

"What are you talking about?"

"The access to Daniel's computer," she said, still typing. "It wasn't just to monitor my 'revenge project,' was it? You used him as cover, routing your other activities through his IP address.

Clever. If anyone traced the suspicious financial transactions, they'd lead to a crime novelist with an active imagination, not a dead man."

Michael set down his wineglass slowly. "You're reaching, Mira."

"Am I?" She held up her phone, showing a series of text messages. "I've been in contact with someone who's very interested in finding you, Michael. Someone who never believed you died in that boating accident."

For the first time since entering the apartment, Michael's composure faltered visibly. "Who?"

"Agent Teresa Kwan, Financial Crimes Division." Mira's voice carried a cold satisfaction. "She's been building a case against you for years. Never could prove you were still alive, though. Until now."

Daniel watched the siblings' standoff, pieces clicking into place.

"The wine," he said suddenly. "You drugged him. Just like you drugged me."

Mira's eyes never left her brother. "It won't knock him out, just make him compliant, slow his reactions. Enough for authorities to take him into custody without incident."

Michael started to rise from his chair, then swayed, gripping the armrest for support. "You... you've been planning this?"

"Since I realized you were alive, about six months ago," Mira confirmed, a grim smile playing at her lips. "I noticed familiar patterns in some financial transactions I was researching for a client. Your patterns, Michael. Always the same elegant structure, the same mathematical ratio in how you moved funds."

She glanced at Daniel. "Moving across from Daniel wasn't about revenge. It was about setting a trap for you. I knew you'd monitor anyone I took a special interest in."

Michael's face contorted with anger and betrayal, but his movements were becoming visibly sluggish. "Family... above all," he managed, his words slurring slightly.

"Yes," Mira agreed coldly. "That's why I'm doing this. For Martin."

She turned to Daniel, her expression softening. "I never drugged you that night. You really did just drink too much wine. Everything else, the remote access, the fabricated evidence, that was all Michael, not me."

Daniel stared at her, struggling to reconcile this new version of events with what he'd believed. "And contacting Patricia? The harassment claims?"

"Real concerns based on your initial observation of me," Mira admitted. "I needed it to seem convincing enough that Michael would believe I was genuinely targeting you. I needed him to see you as a useful pawn, not a threat."

She glanced at her phone as it vibrated with an incoming message. "They're on their way up. Two minutes." Michael made a desperate lunge toward the door, but his movements were uncoordinated, his balance compromised by whatever Mira had put in his wine. He collapsed back into the chair, his face a mask of fury and disbelief.

"You chose... a stranger... over your own blood," he slurred, glaring at Mira.

"No," she replied quietly. "I chose justice for Martin over protecting his killer." She turned to Daniel as the sound of multiple footsteps became audible in the hallway outside. "I'm sorry for involving you in this. I never intended it to affect you the way it did."

Daniel removed the voice recorder from his pocket, stopping the recording. "I still don't understand. If you knew it was Michael all along, why not just tell me?"

"Because I wasn't certain you weren't working with him," Mira admitted. "Not until I saw your genuine confusion tonight. Michael has always been persuasive, manipulative. I couldn't risk him knowing I was onto him."

A sharp knock at the door interrupted them. "Federal agents! Open up!" As Mira moved to answer the door, Daniel tried to process the dizzying series of revelations. The writer that he was, he'd been outplayed by a more complex plot than he could have imagined.

The door burst open with a thunderous crack, hinges protesting as it slammed against the wall. Silhouetted in the harsh hallway light stood a tactical team in full gear, ballistic vests emblazoned with "FEDERAL AGENT" across the chest, utility belts weighted with equipment, and sidearms held at the ready position. Their movements were choreographed with practiced precision, each agent flowing into the apartment with swift, controlled steps.

At their head strode a woman Daniel presumed was Agent Kwan. She was slim but commanding in a charcoal pantsuit that seemed to absorb what little light remained in the room. Her dark hair was pulled back into a severe bun, emphasizing sharp cheekbones and eyes that missed nothing. A thin silver chain disappeared beneath her collar, the only personal touch in her otherwise impeccable federal appearance.

"Secure the suspect," she ordered, her voice clipped and authoritative, betraying only the slightest hint of an accent. Two agents immediately broke formation to approach Michael, who slumped against the wall, his eyes unfocused and half-lidded. A thin trickle of blood had dried along his temple, disappearing into his disheveled hair.

The room transformed in seconds; corners checked, closets opened, equipment unpacked. Tactical flashlights cut through the apartment's gloom, creating stark shadows that danced across the walls. The agents moved with the synchronized efficiency of those who had done this dozens of times before, their boots barely making a sound on the worn carpet.

Michael's head lolled to one side as the agents carefully but firmly secured his wrists with reinforced zip ties. His mumbled protests were barely audible over the controlled chaos of the raid. The apartment, which had moments ago felt claustrophobic in its stillness, now seemed impossibly small with the presence of the tactical team.

Agent Kwan surveyed the scene, her expression revealing nothing as she took in the disheveled state of the apartment. Papers scattered across the coffee table, half-empty mugs growing cold, the faint scent of desperation that had permeated the space long before they'd arrived. When she finally turned her attention to Daniel, her gaze was calculating, assessing him with the cool detachment of someone who had long ago learned to separate emotion from duty.

The fluorescent hallway light created a halo effect around her silhouette, leaving her face in shadow. Behind her, the team continued their methodical takeover of the small apartment, transforming the intimate space into an extension of federal authority with each passing second.

"Mira Voss?" the lead agent asked.

Mira nodded. "Thank you for coming so quickly."

"We've been waiting for this moment for a long time," Agent Kwan replied, watching as her team handcuffed Michael. She turned her attention to Daniel. "And you are?"

"Daniel Mercer," he answered, still feeling as if he'd stepped into someone else's story. "I'm... a neighbor."

Agent Kwan studied him briefly. "We'll need statements from both of you."

As the agents prepared to remove Michael from the apartment, Mira approached Daniel. "When this is over," she said quietly, "I'd like to tell you the real story about Martin. Not the one you wrote, not the one Michael created. The truth."

Daniel looked at her, this woman he'd observed, fictionalized, feared, and completely misunderstood. "I'd like that," he replied. "I think I owe him that much."

Outside the apartment, the city continued its nighttime rhythm, oblivious to the drama that had unfolded within these walls. Daniel thought about his manuscript waiting across the street, the story that had seemed so clear just hours ago, now revealed as a pale shadow of a much more complex reality.

As a writer, he'd always prided himself on his insight, his ability to see the truth behind human behavior. Now he understood how little he actually knew, how stories, even those we tell ourselves, are always incomplete, always shaped by perspectives we cannot fully see.

The real chapter was only beginning.

CHAPTER 8: START OF END

The next twelve hours passed in a blur of statements, questioning, and revelations. Daniel and Mira found themselves in separate rooms at the FBI field office, recounting their versions of events to agents who received each outlandish turn with professional stoicism. When Daniel finally emerged from his third interview of the morning, exhausted and coffee-saturated, he found Mira waiting in the reception area, looking similarly drained.

"They're done with you?" he asked, collapsing into the chair beside her.

She nodded; her eyes fixed on some middle distance. "For now. Michael's not talking yet, but they have enough to hold him while they build the case." She turned to look at him. "They found the hidden partition on your computer. The files he planted were... severe."

Daniel exhaled slowly. "Agent Kwan told me. Child exploitation material. He really was setting me up for destruction."

"Michael never does things halfway," Mira said, a bitter edge to her voice. "He wanted insurance that you'd pay without question." She hesitated before adding, "I'm sorry you were pulled into this. Truly."

"I still don't understand everything," Daniel admitted. "Why did you approach me at the café that day? Why invite me to dinner if you suspected Michael was watching?"

Mira rubbed her eyes, the gesture making her seem suddenly vulnerable. "I needed to confirm my suspicions. I knew if Michael was alive and monitoring me, he'd make a move once he saw me getting close to you, a potential asset he could exploit."

"So, I was bait," Daniel said, not accusingly but with dawning comprehension.

"Initially," she acknowledged. "But then..." She paused, searching for words. "Things got complicated." Before Daniel could ask what she meant, Agent Kwan appeared, her crisp suit somehow unwrinkled despite what must have been a sleepless night.

"Mr. Mercer, Ms. Voss," she addressed them both, "we've made significant progress on Mr. Voss's financial network based on the information you've provided. I want to thank you both for your cooperation."

"What happens now?" Daniel asked.

"We continue building our case," Kwan replied. "The evidence on your computer has been documented and removed. We'll need you both to remain available for further questions, but you're free to go home for now." She handed them each a card. "Call me directly if you remember anything else that might be relevant."

When they finally left the federal building, morning had given way to afternoon, the October sun casting long shadows across the city streets. They stood awkwardly on the sidewalk, the shared ordeal creating an unexpected intimacy neither seemed quite ready to acknowledge.

"I should get some sleep," Mira said finally.

"So should I," Daniel agreed. "But I don't think I can. Not yet." He hesitated. "You mentioned telling me the real story about Martin."

Something softened in Mira's expression. "I did."

"I'd still like to hear it. If you're willing."

She considered him for a long moment. "There's a diner two blocks from here. They make decent coffee."

"Lead the way," Daniel said.

The diner was sparsely populated at this odd hour between lunch and dinner. They claimed a corner booth away from other patrons, ordered coffee, and sat in silence until the waitress had come and gone.

"Where should I start?" Mira asked, wrapping her hands around the warm mug.

"The beginning," Daniel suggested. "Who was Martin, really?"

Mira's gaze turned inward, accessing memories that seemed to bring both pain and fondness. "Martin was the middle child. Sensitive. Brilliant with numbers and patterns but awkward with people. He idolized Michael, who was everything Martin wasn't, confident, charismatic, socially adept."

She took a sip of coffee before continuing. "Our father was... demanding. Old-world values about family and loyalty above all else. Michael thrived under that pressure. Martin crumbled. I survived by keeping emotional distance."

"And the case I wrote about?" Daniel prompted it gently.

"Kimberly Renner," Mira nodded. "Your book got some things right. She and Martin were involved briefly. She disappeared after their breakup. The evidence did point to him."

"But?"

"But Martin wasn't capable of the calculating behavior you described in your book. The methodical planning, the careful execution." She met Daniel's eyes directly. "That was Michael's signature."

Daniel felt a chill. "You think Michael killed her?" "I know he did," Mira said with quiet certainty. "Not directly, Michael never gets his hands dirty. But he arranged it when she became a liability."

"A liability, how?"

"Kim worked at the same investment firm as Michael. Junior position, but smart. She started dating Martin after meeting him at a company event." Mira's expression darkened. "What none of us knew then was that Michael was already running his schemes, using client funds, manipulating accounts. Kim noticed discrepancies. Mentioned them to Martin because she was worried about getting blamed."

"And Martin told Michael," Daniel concluded, the pieces falling into place.

"Family loyalty above all," Mira confirmed bitterly. "Martin never imagined Michael would... handle it the way he did. When Kim disappeared and evidence pointed to Martin, he was genuinely shocked, devastated."

"But he didn't come forward," Daniel observed.

"He couldn't process the betrayal. Couldn't accept that his beloved brother would set him up as a potential murder suspect." She shook her head sadly. "By the time the investigation cleared him due to lack of concrete evidence, Martin was broken. Your book was just the final straw."

Daniel sat back, absorbing this. "And Michael's fake death?"

"The investigations were getting too close. Multiple agencies were looking into the firm's activities. Michael needed to disappear." Mira's voice hardened. "He convinced Martin to help him fake his death, promised he'd send for him once he was established somewhere safe. Instead, he used Martin to handle his remaining affairs, transfer assets, cover his tracks. When Martin was no longer useful..."

"He abandoned him," Daniel finished.

"Worse," Mira said. "He started withdrawing the emotional support that had kept Martin functioning. The late-night calls stopped. The reassurances disappeared. He knew exactly what that would do to Martin, who had sacrificed everything for him."

Daniel thought about his portrayal of Martin in his book. He had shown Martin as a cold, calculating figure which he'd constructed based on circumstantial evidence and his own imagination. How utterly wrong he had been.

"I should have dug deeper," he said quietly. "Asked more questions."

"You couldn't have known," Mira replied. "Michael is very good at constructing narratives, controlling information. We all believed what he wanted us to believe for years."

"How did you figure it out? That he was still alive?"

"After Martin died, I went through his things. Found encrypted communications, fragments of information that didn't make sense unless Michael was still out there somewhere." Her expression turned grimmer. "Then I started working with a financial forensics firm. Specialized in tracking hidden assets in divorce cases, corporate disputes. I got good at recognizing patterns, following money trails. Six months ago, I spotted something familiar, a transaction structure I'd seen in Martin's records."

"And you set up this elaborate plan to catch him," Daniel said, still processing the scope of her operation.

"I knew if he thought I was focused on something else, like getting revenge on you, he'd be less careful around me." Mira looked genuinely regretful. "I never intended to cause you actual harm. The conversation with your agent was meant to establish a believable pattern of concern, nothing more."

Daniel thought back to his manuscript, to all his theories about Mira's motivations. "I thought I understood what was happening. I thought I had the story figured out."

"Writers," Mira said with a hint of a smile. "Always imposing story, where sometimes there's just chaos."

"Not chaos," Daniel countered. "Just a different story than the one I was telling myself."

They lapsed into silence, the weight of shared revelation settling between them. Outside, the afternoon had begun its gradual surrender to evening, streetlights flickering on one by one.

"What now?" Daniel finally asked.

"I will testify against Michael when the time comes," Mira replied. "Try to make amends for Martin in whatever way I can."

"And us?" The question escaped before Daniel could consider its implications.

Mira studied him, something complicated moving behind her eyes. "I'm not sure there is an 'us,' Daniel. Our connection was built on false premises, manipulations."

"Not entirely," he ventured. "There was something real at that dinner, before everything went sideways. At least, it felt real to me."

A small, genuine smile softened her features. "It did to me too. That was the complication."

Daniel hesitated, then reached across the table, his hand stopping just short of hers. "Maybe we could start over. No observations, no revenge plots, no manipulative brothers. Just two people who've been through something extraordinary together."

Mira looked at his outstretched hand, then back to his face. "I'm not sure that's possible. There's too much between us."

"Perhaps," Daniel acknowledged. "Or perhaps that's just another narrative we're telling ourselves because it's safer than the alternative."

Her eyebrow rose slightly. "Which is?"

"That sometimes connections form in the strangest circumstances. That trauma can be a crucible as well as a wound." He smiled tentatively. "That two people who've seen each other at their most vulnerable might actually have a head start on something honest."

Mira didn't reach for his hand, but she didn't pull away either. "You're a hopeless romantic for someone who writes such dark thrillers."

"Occupational hazard," he admitted. "I see potential stories everywhere."

"And what story do you see here?"

Daniel considered the question carefully. "I see two people who thought they understood each other based on appearances and assumptions, only to discover they knew nothing at all. I see a mystery that's just beginning rather than ending."

"That sounds dangerously like a sequel," Mira observed, but there was warmth in her voice.

"I prefer to think of it as a fresh start," Daniel replied. "A different genre entirely."

Finally, Mira's hand moved across the table to meet his, the touch tentative but deliberate. "I'd like to read that version," she said quietly.

Outside the diner windows, the city continued its endless rhythm, people passing, lives intersecting briefly before continuing on separate trajectories. But inside this small bubble of shared understanding, something new was taking shape, a story neither of them could have anticipated nor written alone.

Daniel thought about his manuscript waiting at home, the narrative that had seemed so clear, so certain in its conclusions. He would set it aside, he decided. Some stories needed to be lived before they could be written.

CHAPTER 9: COMING CLOSE

Three weeks later, Daniel sat at his desk, staring at the blinking cursor on a blank document. His publisher had been surprisingly understanding about the delay on his manuscript, especially after Patricia explained the extraordinary circumstances in carefully redacted form. The involvement of federal authorities in financial crimes tended to make deadlines seem suddenly flexible.

The morning sun filtered through partially open blinds, casting warm stripes across his workspace. Daniel had kept them that way since the night of Michael's arrest, neither fully closed in paranoia nor completely open in careless vulnerability. A middle ground that felt right for now.

His phone buzzed with a text from Mira: Still meeting at 11? I have something to show you.

He smiled slightly, typing back: I'll be there. The usual place?

Her response came quickly: Yes. Don't be late. This is important.

Their relationship, if it could be called that, had evolved cautiously over the past weeks. Coffee meetings, carefully neutral conversations, the slow build of trust between two people who had seen each other at both their worst and most vulnerable. Neither rushing toward nor retreating from whatever this connection might become.

At exactly 11 AM, Daniel arrived at the small bookshop café where they'd established their routine. Mira was already there, a leather portfolio on the table beside her coffee. She looked different somehow, more present, less guarded. The careful observer in him noticed how she no longer positioned herself with her back to the wall, no longer scanned each new customer who entered with subtle vigilance.

"Right on time," she said as he approached. "Very unlike a writer."

"I'm turning over a new leaf," Daniel replied, settling into the chair across from her. "Punctuality, sobriety, general emotional stability, all the boring virtues."

That earned a smile. "How's the new manuscript coming?"

"It isn't," he admitted. "I've been staring at a blank page for days."

"Writer's block?"

"More like writer's recalibration." Daniel paused as the barista delivered his usual Americano. "Everything I thought I knew about constructing narratives, about understanding people's motivations... it all seems naive now."

Mira studied him thoughtfully. "That sounds like growth, not failure."

"Maybe," he acknowledged. "But publishers generally prefer pages over personal epiphanies."

"Speaking of pages," Mira said, patting the leather portfolio, "that's why I asked to meet today. I have something you should see."

She opened the portfolio and removed a bound manuscript, its cover page bearing a simple title: The Invisible Thread by Martin Voss.

Daniel stared at it, momentarily speechless. "Is that..."

"Martin's unpublished manuscript," Mira confirmed. "The one you asked about that night in my apartment."

"I was bluffing," Daniel admitted. "I had no idea it actually existed."

"Sometimes a writer's intuition is more accurate than they realize." She pushed the manuscript toward him. "I found it among his things after his death. I've never shown it to anyone else."

Daniel hesitated before touching it, understanding the significance of the gesture. "Why now? Why show me?"

"Because you wanted to know who Martin really was," she said simply. "This tells that story better than I ever could."

He placed his hand on the manuscript, feeling the weight of it—both physical and metaphorical. "Have you read it?"

"Many times." Something vulnerable flickered across Mira's features. "It's not what you might expect. It's not a confession or an accusation. It's fiction, but like all good fiction..."

"It contains deeper truths," Daniel finished.

"Exactly."

Daniel opened to the first page, reading the dedication: *For those who bear witness, even when the story seems impossible to believe.*

"He wrote it in the months before his suicide," Mira explained. "After Michael's 'death,' during the period when your book was gaining popularity."

"Does it address the Kimberly case?" Daniel prodded.

"Not directly. It's about two brothers, one brilliant but fragile, the other charismatic but empty inside. About family loyalty pushed to destructive extremes." She traced her finger lightly along the edge of the manuscript. "About what happens when we build our identity around someone else's narrative."

Daniel closed the cover, understanding he couldn't properly absorb such a document in a casual café setting. "Thank you for trusting me with this."

"I'm not giving it to you," Mira clarified. "I'm sharing it. There's a difference."

"Of course," Daniel nodded. The distinction mattered.

"I have a proposal," she continued, her tone shifting to something more businesslike. "A collaboration of sorts."

"I'm listening."

"Martin's story deserves to be told, the real story, not the one constructed by Michael, not the one in your book, not even my version." Her eyes met his directly. "I think we should write it together. A non-fiction account of what actually happened, incorporating sections of Martin's manuscript where relevant."

Daniel hadn't expected this. "You want to co-author a book with me?"

"Who better? You have the narrative skills and publishing connections. I have the insider knowledge and Martin's work." She leaned forward slightly. "More importantly, we both have a stake in getting this right. In correcting the record."

Daniel considered the proposition carefully. His publisher would certainly be interested; the story had all the elements of a bestseller. But the ethical considerations were complex.

"What about Michael's trial? The ongoing investigation?"

"We work with the authorities, get necessary clearances," Mira replied, having clearly thought this through. "Agent Kwan has already indicated they might be amenable, especially since it could potentially bring forward other victims of Michael's schemes."

"And Martin's manuscript? Are you comfortable with sections being published?"

"It's what he would have wanted," Mira said with quiet certainty. "He wrote it to be read, to be understood. Not by everyone, perhaps, but by someone who could recognize the truth in it."

Daniel thought about his stalled new manuscript, his inability to return to the kind of facile character construction that had once come so easily. Perhaps this was the project he needed, not just professionally but personally. A chance to use his skills for revelation rather than exploitation, for truth rather than marketable fiction.

"I'd want to approach it differently than my previous work," he said finally. "More transparency about sources, more acknowledgment of ambiguity where facts can't be verified."

"That's exactly what I want too," Mira agreed. "No more creating convenient narratives at the expense of complex truths."

Daniel extended his hand across the table. "Then I think we have a deal."

Mira took his hand, the handshake firm and purposeful. But as she began to withdraw, Daniel gently maintained his hold.

"This doesn't have to be just professional," he said quietly.

Her expression softened. "I know. But let's start there. The rest... has time to develop naturally. Without expectations or preconceptions."

"Without any judgements?" Daniel suggested with a small smile.

"Exactly." She squeezed his hand once before releasing it. "We've both had enough of other people's stories for a while."

As they left the café together, the manuscript securely returned to Mira's portfolio, Daniel felt something he hadn't experienced since before this entire ordeal began; creative purpose. Not the frantic energy of deadlines or the competitive drive for bestseller lists, but something more substantial, the desire to use his talents for illumination rather than manipulation.

They walked without hurry through the crisp autumn afternoon, discussing practical aspects of their collaboration, sketching the broad outline of the project ahead. Two people who had begun as observer and subject, evolved to opponent and target, and now stood as potential partners in something neither could fully predict.

The story was still unfolding, but for once, Daniel was content to experience it rather than control it, to be a participant rather than merely the author.

CHAPTER 10: JUDGEMENTS

The federal courthouse loomed against a slate-gray December sky, its stone facade imposing and austere. Daniel adjusted his tie, uncomfortable in the formal attire he rarely wore, and glanced at Mira beside him on the courthouse steps.

"Ready?" he asked.

She nodded; her face composed but tension evident in the set of her shoulders. "As I'll ever be."

Today marked the beginning of pretrial motions in United States v. Michael Voss. After weeks of investigation, the prosecution had assembled a formidable case, financial fraud, tax evasion, conspiracy, obstruction of justice, and most seriously, solicitation of murder in Kimberly Renner's disappearance. Michael had maintained his innocence on all charges, his charisma and performative indignation apparently undiminished by incarceration.

They weren't required to be here today; their testimonies wouldn't be needed until the trial proper. But Mira had wanted to witness these initial proceedings, to see her brother in the stark reality of a courtroom rather than the dramatic flair of his unexpected appearance in her apartment. Daniel had offered to accompany her without hesitation.

Inside, they found seats at the back of the courtroom. The space was only half-filled, mostly journalists, legal interns, and a few curious members of the public drawn by the sensational elements of the case. Financial crimes rarely attracted attention unless they were attached to more visceral charges.

"There's Agent Kwan," Daniel murmured, nodding toward the severe-looking woman conferring with the prosecution team. Mira acknowledged this with a tight nod but said nothing. Her focus had narrowed to the side door through which defendants were brought in from holding.

When it finally opened and Michael appeared, flanked by marshals and followed by his defense attorney, Daniel felt Mira stiffen beside him. Michael was impeccably dressed in a tailored suit that somehow maintained its sharp lines despite his circumstances. His confident stride and easy smile suggested a man attending a business meeting rather than facing multiple felony charges.

As Michael took his seat at the defense table, his gaze swept the courtroom in what seemed like casual interest until it landed on Mira and Daniel. For a fleeting moment, something cold and calculating replaced his pleasant expression before the mask slipped back into place. He offered a small nod of acknowledgment, as if they were distant acquaintances crossing paths at a social function.

Mira didn't respond, her face deliberately impassive. Daniel recognized the self-protective blankness he'd once misinterpreted as calculation or manipulation. Now he understood it was armor, carefully constructed and maintained.

The proceedings themselves were technical and brief. It started with discussions of evidence discovery timelines, motion filing deadlines, and preliminary arguments about jurisdictional matters. Throughout, Michael maintained an engaged, thoughtful demeanor, occasionally leaning to whisper something to his attorney, who appeared far more concerned than his client.

When the judge called a brief recess, Michael rose and, to Daniel's surprise, approached them directly, his attorney hurrying after him with a concerned expression.

"Mira," Michael greeted her, his voice warm as if they were meeting for a family dinner. "I'm glad you came." His gaze shifted to Daniel. "Mr. Mercer. Still keeping interesting company, I see."

"Mr. Voss, I advised against this," his attorney murmured urgently.

Michael waved him off. "My sister and I are just having a civil conversation. Nothing improper about that."

Mira remained seated, her posture rigid. "What do you want, Michael?"

"To understand," he replied, his expression shifting to something that might have passed for hurt on someone with actual emotional capacity. "Family loyalty above all, that was always our code. And yet here you are, aligned with a stranger against your own blood."

"Don't," Mira said quietly. "Don't try to manipulate this into something about betrayal. You destroyed Martin. You tried to destroy Daniel. You would have destroyed me too if it served your purposes."

Michael's smile dimmed only slightly. "Such dramatics, You should have been an actress. Martin was troubled long before anything I did. And Mr. Mercer here," he glanced at Daniel with something like amusement, "was merely a contingency plan. Business, nothing personal."

"Framing someone for child exploitation is very personal," Daniel said evenly.

"An unfortunate necessity," Michael replied with a casual shrug. "Insurance policies are rarely pleasant to contemplate but essential nonetheless."

His attorney placed a hand on his arm. "Mr. Voss, I must insist...."

"One moment, Richard," Michael said, his focus returning to Mira. "I hear you're working on a book together. How enterprising of you both."

Mira's expression betrayed nothing. "You have spies?."

"Yes, I still have friends in interesting places," Michael replied. His tone remained conversational, but something harder entered his eyes. "I wonder if you've considered the family implications of airing such personal history publicly."

"Are you threatening me?" Mira asked directly.

"Threatening? No." You always misunderstand me, Michael's smile returned, pleasant and utterly false. "Merely expressing fraternal concern about potential repercussions. Some narratives, once released, can't be controlled."

Daniel felt a chill at the calculated menace beneath the cordial exterior.

Before he could respond, a marshal approached. "Sir, you need to return to your seat. Recess is ending."

Michael nodded agreeably. "Of course." He turned back to Mira. "Think about what I said, sister. There's still time to reconsider your approach here."

As he walked away, his attorney lingering only long enough to mutter "No further contact, please" before hurrying after his client, Daniel turned to Mira.

"You okay?"

She exhaled slowly. "I knew he'd try something like this. He's realizing his usual tactics aren't working, so he's getting desperate."

"What did he mean about repercussions?"

"Nothing specific," Mira replied, though her expression suggested otherwise. "Just typical Michael; vague threats designed to make you imagine the worst."

The judge returned, and proceedings resumed. They stayed through the remainder of the session, watching as dates were set and preliminary matters resolved. Michael did not look their way again, maintaining his focus on the legal proceedings with apparent attentiveness.

When it was over and they finally emerged into the winter afternoon, fat snowflakes had begun drifting from the leaden sky, dusting the courthouse steps with white. The temperature had dropped sharply, the cold air biting at exposed skin. "Let's get out of here," Mira said, pulling her coat tighter.

They walked in silence for a block before Daniel spoke. "He's still trying to control you."

"That's what Michael does," Mira replied. "He's always been the author of our family's story."

"Not anymore," Daniel said firmly. "That's what our book is about, telling the truth no matter how complex or messy."

Mira glanced at him, a hint of her usual wry humor returning. "Very noble. Also, potentially very naïve."

"Probably," Daniel admitted. "But I'd rather be naïvely committed to truth than cynically skilled at manipulation."

"When did you get so principled?" she asked, but there was warmth in her voice.

"Around the time I realized how thoroughly I'd been played," he replied with a self-deprecating smile.

"Nothing like complete humiliation to inspire ethical reflection."

They reached the corner where they would normally part ways, Mira to her temporary apartment across town. She'd moved out of the unit across from Daniel's, both of them agreeing the proximity carried too many complicated associations. Daniel went back to his office where their manuscript was taking shape.

But something in Michael's veiled threats had left Daniel unsettled.

"Come back to my place," he said impulsively. "We can work on the book there. I don't like the idea of you being alone right now."

Mira raised her eyebrow. "I've been dealing with Michael's manipulations my entire life. I can handle a few vague threats."

"I know you can," Daniel acknowledged. "That's not the point."

"What is the point?"

Daniel considered his answer carefully. "The point is that neither of us has to handle things alone anymore. Isn't that what we've been learning through this whole ordeal?"

Mira studied him for a long moment as snowflakes caught in her dark hair. "You're getting dangerously close to me again," she said, but her expression had softened.

"Maybe," he conceded. "Or maybe I'm just suggesting we write the next chapter together, rather than separately."

A small smile formed at the corners of her mouth. "That was either deep or incredibly corny."

"Why not both?" Daniel returned her smile. "The best truths often are."

Mira shook her head in mock exasperation, but when Daniel held out his hand, she took it without hesitation.

"Fine," she said. "But I get to choose dinner. Your taste in takeout is appalling."

As they made their way through the steadily falling snow, Daniel felt a sense of cautious optimism. The road ahead remained complex, Michael's trial, the book they were creating, their own evolving relationship, but for the first time in months, the story felt authentic rather than manipulated.

CHAPTER 11: UNEXPECTED TERRAIN

Snow continued to fall as they reached Daniel's apartment, transforming the city into something quieter, more contemplative. He fumbled with his keys, fingers stiff from the cold, while Mira waited beside him, snowflakes melting in her dark hair.

"I forgot how much I hate winter," she remarked, rubbing her gloved hands together. Daniel pushed the door open.

"Says the woman who chose to live in Chicago for three years."

"A decision made purely for academic reasons, not meteorological ones." She stepped inside, unwinding her scarf. "My relationship with weather is complicated."

"Like all your relationships?" Daniel asked, immediately regretting the words. They'd developed a careful rapport over the past weeks, professionals with undercurrents of something deeper neither had been willing to articulate.

To his relief, Mira smiled. "Precisely like that."

The apartment looked different than when she'd last seen it. Gone were the scattered notes and chaotic piles of research materials. In their place stood a large corkboard covered with an intricate timeline of events, color-coded sticky notes, and photographs connected by red string.

"Very detective movie of you," Mira observed, moving closer to examine it.

"I needed to visualize everything." Daniel shrugged off his coat. "Helped me see patterns I was missing before."

Mira studied the board. "You've been busy."

"The book won't write itself," he replied, watching her. "Though some days I wish it would."

They ordered Thai food, Mira's choice, and settled at his dining table with laptops open and notes spread between them. This had become their routine: collaborative writing sessions punctuated by debates over structure, phrasing, and which truths deserved priority. What began as tense interactions had evolved into something more fluid, their respective strengths complementing each other.

Daniel was direct, journalistic, concerned with factual accuracy. Mira brought psychological depth and contextual understanding. Together, they were crafting something neither could have produced alone.

"How much should we include about today?" Daniel asked, fingers hovering over his keyboard.

Mira took a sip from her tea before answering. "All of it. Michael's veiled threats, his attempt to manipulate me using family loyalty, it's textbook behavior for him."

"You weren't intimidated," Daniel observed.

"No." She paused. "But I was affected. There's a difference."

Daniel's phone buzzed with a notification from the delivery app. He excused himself to collect their food, returning minutes later to find Mira standing before his bookshelf, holding a framed photograph he'd almost forgotten was there.

"Your sister?" she asked.

Daniel set the food containers on the coffee table. "Yeah. Ellie. Taken about a year before she died." The photograph showed a young woman with Daniel's same warm eyes, sitting cross-legged on a beach at sunset, laughing at something beyond the frame. The kind of candid moment that captures a person's essence.

"She looks happy," Mira said quietly.

"She was, that day." Daniel moved beside her. "Not always, but she had good moments. That's partly why I became a journalist, trying to understand complex truths."

Mira replaced the photograph carefully. "Is that what we're doing with this book? Seeking complex truths?"

"I hope so." Daniel gestured toward the food. "Shall we eat while it's hot?"

They settled on the couch, balancing containers of pad Thai and green curry. For a while, they ate in comfortable silence, the snow outside creating a sense of isolation from the world beyond the windows. "I've been thinking about what Michael said," Mira finally said. "About narratives that can't be controlled once released."

Daniel set down his chopsticks. "Do you think he has actual leverage, or is he just trying to get in your head?"

"Both," she admitted. "There are things I haven't told you yet. Things about our family that... complicate matters."

"Is this related to what happened to your parents?"

Mira's expression closed slightly. "Yes. But also, about Martin, and other family situations that Michael could potentially twist." She placed her half-finished food on the coffee table. "I need to decide how much I'm willing to expose."

"You don't have to tell me everything," Daniel said carefully.

"For the book to work, I might have to." Her gaze met his.

"That's what scares me."

"What are you afraid of?" he asked. "Michael's retaliation?"

"No." She hesitated. "I'm afraid of how you'll see me once you know everything."

The admission hung between them, more intimate than anything that had passed between them before. Daniel set his own food aside and turned to face her fully. "Mira," he said quietly, "whatever you tell me won't change what I already know about you."

"You can't promise that."

"I can," he insisted. "Because I've seen who you are in the moments when there's nothing to gain from pretense."

She looked away, studying the falling snow beyond the window.

"You have a remarkable capacity for believing in people despite evidence to the contrary."

"Only when they deserve it." Her smile was tinged with sadness.

"Your sister was lucky to have you."

"I failed her," Daniel said simply.

"How?"

He hadn't planned to share this, hadn't discussed Ellie's struggles with anyone in years. But something about Mira's presence, the liminal quality of the snow-muffled afternoon, made honesty feel not just possible but necessary.

"I was so focused on understanding her illness that I missed seeing her," he explained. "I wanted to fix everything, find the right combination of treatment and support that would bring back the sister I remembered. I was looking for a solution when I should have been looking at Ellie."

Mira's expression softened. "That's not failure, Daniel. That's human."

"Maybe." He shrugged. "But it taught me something I've carried into every relationship since; people aren't puzzles to solve. They're landscapes to explore."

"That's a generous interpretation of what I've put you through," Mira said wryly.

"I didn't say the landscapes were always pleasant," Daniel replied with a small smile.

"Sometimes they're treacherous terrain." Mira laughed then, a genuine sound that transformed her face. Daniel realized he'd rarely heard it before, and something inside him shifted at the recognition.

"So," she said, composing herself, "you're exploring treacherous terrain with me?"

"I'd say we're exploring it together at this point." Their eyes met, and the moment expanded, filled with possibilities neither had allowed themselves to consider fully. Daniel found himself acutely aware of her proximity, the subtle scent of her perfume, the way the lamplight caught the angles of her face.

Mira broke the silence first. "We should get back to work."

"Right," Daniel agreed, though neither of them moved immediately.

When they finally returned to their laptops, something had changed between them, a barrier lowered, a distance shortened. They worked late into the evening, their writing flowing more naturally than before, words building upon each other in organic harmony.

Outside, the snow continued to fall, insulating them from the world beyond Daniel's apartment. By midnight, exhaustion caught up with them both, and Daniel insisted Mira take his bed while he slept on the couch.

"This is unnecessary," she protested. "I can get a rideshare home."

"In this weather? At this hour?" Daniel shook his head. "That's absurd."

"I'm not taking your bed," she countered.

"Then we're at an impasse." He crossed his arms. "I'm too tired to argue creatively."

In the end, they compromised, Mira on the couch despite Daniel's objections, supplied with spare blankets and pillows that smelled faintly of his laundry detergent. As she settled in, Daniel paused in the hallway.

"You know," he said quietly, "whatever you decide to share about your family about anything it's your choice. The book needs truth, but not at the expense of your wellbeing."

Mira looked up at him, her expression unguarded in a way he'd rarely seen. "Thank you," she said simply.

"Goodnight, Mira."

"Goodnight, Daniel."

Morning arrived with startling brightness, sunlight reflecting off fresh snow and pouring through Daniel's windows. He found Mira already awake, standing at his corkboard with a mug of coffee cradled in her hands. "I made coffee," she said without turning. "Hope that's okay."

"More than okay," Daniel replied, shuffling to the kitchen to pour himself a cup. "You sleep alright?"

"Better than expected." She turned to face him, her expression resolute.

"I've made a decision. About what to include in the book."

Daniel took a careful sip from his mug. "I'm listening."

"Everything," Mira said simply. "The full truth about our family, about my parents' deaths, about Martin's involvement. All of it."

"Are you sure? Once it's published...."

"I know," she interrupted. "But Michael was right about one thing, stories have power. I'm tired of letting his version be the only one that exists."

Daniel nodded slowly. "Okay. Then that's what we'll do."

"It won't be easy," she warned. "Some of it will be... difficult to hear. And to write."

"Most important things are," he replied.

They spent the morning at his dining table, Mira speaking, Daniel listening and occasionally asking clarifying questions. She revealed the full story of her parents' deaths, not the accident reported in official records. It was a complex tragedy stemming from her father's gambling debts and her mother's subsequent depression. How Michael had manipulated both situations to his advantage, positioning himself as the family savior while orchestrating much of the financial ruin that preceded their deaths.

She explained Martin's role, not merely as Michael's victim but initially his willing accomplice. He was drawn in by the promise of wealth and importance before realizing the moral compromises required. By then, he was too entangled to escape without legal consequences.

Daniel listened without judgment, watching Mira transform as she spoke, becoming not lighter, exactly, but more integrated. He could see the compartmentalized parts of herself merging into a more coherent whole.

When she finally finished, late afternoon shadows stretching across the apartment, she looked drained but present in a way Daniel hadn't seen before.

"Thank you," he said simply, "for trusting me with this."

Mira tucked a strand of hair behind her ear, a rare gesture of uncertainty. "It's strange. I've spent so long carrying these secrets, I'd forgotten how heavy they were until I set them down."

Daniel reached across the table and covered her hand with his own. She didn't pull away.

"We should get this written while it's fresh," he suggested gently. Mira nodded, but didn't immediately open her laptop. Instead, she turned her hand beneath his so their palms met, fingers intertwining.

"Before we do," she said quietly, "there's something else I need to address."

Daniel waited, heart beating faster than he cared to admit. "This," she continued, gesturing between them with her free hand. "Us. Whatever is happening here."

"Is something happening here?" Daniel asked, his tone deliberately light despite the significance of the question.

"Don't be obtuse," Mira replied, but there was no edge to her words. "You know there is."

"I know there could be," he corrected. "If we wanted it."

"Do you?" she asked directly. "Want it?"

Daniel considered deflecting, they had the book to finish, Michael's trial was approaching, timing was impossible but found himself unwilling to hide behind practicalities.

"Yes," he said simply. "I do."

Mira's expression remained serious. "You realize how complicated this makes everything."

"I suspect 'complicated' is our natural state," Daniel replied. "Might as well embrace it."

A smile tugged at her lips. "That's an alarmingly healthy perspective."

"I have my moments."

Without releasing his hand, Mira stood and moved around the table until she stood beside his chair. Daniel rose to face her, their proximity suddenly charged with potential.

"This could be a terrible mistake," she murmured.

"Possibly," he agreed. "We have a talent for those."

"Speak for yourself," she replied, and then closed the distance between them.

The kiss was hesitant at first, questioning, before deepening into something more certain. Daniel's hands found her waist as hers moved to his shoulders, the contact grounding them both in the reality of this unexpected shift.

When they finally separated, Mira's expression was uncharacteristically vulnerable. "We still have to finish the book."

"We will," Daniel assured her. "This doesn't change that."

"It changes everything," she corrected. "But maybe that's not a bad thing."

Before Daniel could respond, his phone rang with an unfamiliar number. He almost ignored it, but professional instinct took over.

"Sorry," he said, stepping back reluctantly. "I should check this."

The caller was Agent Kwan from the FBI, her voice terse and urgent.

"Mr. Mercer? There's been a development. Michael Voss was released on bail this morning. Was calling Mira but she did not pick up."

Daniel felt his body go cold. "That's not possible. The judge denied bail yesterday."

"Emergency hearing this morning with a different judge. His attorney submitted new evidence questioning the strength of the prosecution's case, particularly regarding Ms. Renner's disappearance."

"How is that possible?" Daniel demanded, catching Mira's questioning gaze.

"Someone got to a key witness," Agent Kwan replied grimly. "And there have been... political pressures I'm not at a liberty to discuss."

"Where is he now?"

"That's why I'm calling. We have surveillance on him, but I wanted to warn you both directly. He went straight from court to his attorney's office, but we have reason to believe he may attempt contact."

Daniel thanked her for the warning and ended the call, turning to Mira with the news. Her face paled, but her voice remained steady when she spoke.

"He'll come for the manuscript."

"We have digital copies, backups..."

"That's not enough for Michael," she interrupted. "He'll want to destroy the source." Her eyes met his. "We need to move quickly."

Daniel nodded, professional focus returning despite the emotional complexity of moments before. "I'll call my editor, arrange for manuscript security. We should probably both relocate temporarily, somewhere Michael wouldn't think to look."

"I know a place," Mira said, already reaching for her laptop. "Remote enough to finish writing undisturbed, but with sufficient connectivity to stay in touch with Agent Kwan."

As they moved into rapid preparation, downloading files, making calls, packing essential items, Daniel caught Mira's arm gently.

"Are you okay?"

She looked up at him, determination now replacing the vulnerability of earlier. "I spent years running from Michael's influence. I'm done running."

"This isn't running," Daniel assured her. "It's strategic retreat."

A ghost of a smile crossed her face. "How journalistic of you."

"That is how I am." He hesitated.

"About what happened before"

"We'll figure that out too," she interrupted, her expression softening momentarily. "One complicated thing at a time."

Within an hour, they were in Daniel's car heading north out of the city, the manuscript securely backed up and their immediate plans communicated to Agent Kwan. As the urban landscape gave way to rural highways, Mira's hand found Daniel's on the center console.

"I'm not sorry," she said quietly. "About before."

Daniel glanced at her, this complicated woman who had entered his life under false pretenses and somehow become essential to it. "Neither am I."

Ahead of them, the road stretched into uncertainty, Michael free, their book unfinished, their relationship newly transformed. But for the first time in months, Daniel felt something like hope. Not because the path forward was clear, but because they were facing it together.

He realized some landscapes, even treacherous ones, were worth exploring.

CHAPTER 12: CONVERGENCE

The cabin Mira had suggested was nestled in the Michigan woods, two hours north of the city, a weathered but well-maintained structure belonging to an old college friend who used it primarily in summer. In late December, the property stood isolated, the nearest neighbor half a mile down an unplowed dirt road.

"You're sure your friend won't mind?" Daniel asked as he carried their bags inside.

"Maya's in Australia until February," Mira replied, flicking on lights that revealed rustic but comfortable furnishings. "She was relieved someone would check on the place."

The cabin's main room featured exposed wooden beams, a stone fireplace, and large windows overlooking snow-laden pines. A small kitchen occupied one corner, while a narrow staircase led to a loft bedroom. It was cozy without feeling cramped, remote without seeming desolate.

"I didn't know you had friends with vacation properties," Daniel remarked, setting up his laptop on the dining table.

Mira gave him a sidelong glance. "There are still a few things you don't know about me."

"Apparently." He smiled. "Though significantly fewer than a week ago."

They settled into a productive rhythm over the next three days, writing with renewed focus and urgency. The manuscript was taking final shape, not just an exposé of Michael's crimes, but an exploration of manipulation, family dynamics, and the complex interplay between truth and perception. Daniel's journalistic instincts and Mira's psychological insights merged into something neither could have created alone.

Their personal relationship remained in cautious suspension, acknowledged but not fully explored, both tacitly agreeing that completing the book took priority. Still, something had shifted in their interaction, a newfound ease that manifested in casual touches, shared glances, and conversations that flowed without the earlier undercurrents of suspicion or hesitation.

On the fourth day, as a winter storm gathered outside, Agent Kwan called with an update.

"Michael's attorney is pushing for an expedited trial date," she reported. "And he's been meeting with some high-profile media contacts."

Daniel placed the phone on the speaker so Mira could hear. "He's planning his own narrative."

"Almost certainly," Kwan agreed. "His team has requested a gag order on pretrial publicity. If granted, it could impact your book's release timing."

"How long do we have?" Mira asked.

"The hearing is scheduled for Monday morning. Four days from now."

After the call ended, they worked with renewed determination, pausing only for brief meals and even briefer rest. Daniel noticed Mira growing increasingly tense as they approached completion, her focus sharpening to laser precision.

"We're going to make it," he assured her late on the third night, as they reviewed the final chapters.

Mira rubbed her eyes. "It's not just finishing I'm worried about. It's what happens after."

"After?" Daniel prompted when she didn't continue.

She stood and moved to the window, looking out at the snow-shrouded forest. "Michael doesn't lose, Daniel. Ever."

"We've anticipated as much as we can," Daniel replied, joining her at the window. "The manuscript copies, the backup documentation, Agent Kwan's involvement—"

"That's practical preparation," Mira interrupted. "I'm talking about psychological warfare. Michael knows me better than anyone. He knows exactly how to apply pressure."

Daniel studied her profile, illuminated by moonlight reflecting off the snow.

"What aren't you telling me?"

She was silent for so long he thought she might not answer. When she finally spoke, her voice was barely above a whisper.

"He sent a message yesterday. Through an old channel we used to use."

Daniel felt cold that had nothing to do with the winter air. "What kind of message?"

"Coordinates. And a time. Tomorrow at sunset."

"He wants to meet you," Daniel said, understanding immediately. "Alone."

Mira nodded, still facing the window. "It's how we operated in the past. Direct communication, no electronic trail."

"You're not considering going."

It wasn't a question, but Mira's silence provided an answer more definitive than words.

"Mira," Daniel said urgently, "that's exactly what he wants. To isolate you, manipulate you."

"I know what he's doing," she interrupted, finally turning to face him. "But I also know Michael. If I don't go, he'll escalate. People around me will become targets."

"People like me," Daniel realized.

"You. The publisher. Patricia. Even Agent Kwan. Michael believes he's untouchable right now, which makes him more dangerous, not less."

Daniel shook his head. "We need to tell Kwan immediately. Let the FBI handle this."

"And risk Michael disappearing before the trial? He's already prepared for that possibility—offshore accounts, alternate identities. I've seen his contingency plans."

"So, your solution is to walk into an obvious trap?"

"My solution," Mira said evenly, "is to confront him on my terms, not his. Break the pattern of manipulation by acknowledging it directly."

"That's—"

"Risky," she conceded. "But calculated. I know my brother, Daniel. He expects me to either ignore his message or report it. Showing up alone would surprise him."

"Not showing up alone would surprise him more," Daniel countered.

Mira's expression sharpened. "Absolutely not. I'm not putting you in his crosshairs again."

"I'm already there," Daniel pointed out. "Have been since the day I started investigating him."

They argued well into the night, neither willing to concede. By dawn, exhaustion had tempered their disagreement into pragmatic planning. Mira would meet Michael as requested, but with conditions: Daniel would accompany her to the location but remain at a distance, ready to intervene if necessary. They would alert Agent Kwan to the situation but requested she maintain surveillance without direct intervention unless it became necessary.

"I still don't like this," Daniel said as they finalized the manuscript that morning, sending copies to multiple secure locations.

"Neither do I," Mira admitted. "But sometimes the only way past a threat is through it."

They drove separately to the coordinates Michael had provided. It was an abandoned factory on the outskirts of the city, once part of the automotive industry's empire, now a skeletal reminder of industrial decline. Mira parked directly in the lot as instructed, while Daniel positioned his vehicle half a mile away, approaching on foot through the skeletal remains of administrative buildings.

Sunset painted the snow-covered landscape in hues of pink and gold, the beauty matching with the tension Daniel felt as he watched Mira exit her car and stand alone in the vast, empty lot. She looked smaller than he remembered, a solitary figure against the weathered factory façade. For a terrible moment, he questioned the wisdom of their plan.

Then another vehicle appeared, a black SUV with tinted windows that pulled alongside Mira's car. Michael emerged, impeccably dressed despite the surroundings.

From his position behind a crumbling wall, Daniel couldn't hear their exchange, but he could see their body language clearly. Michael stood with practiced ease; hands open in apparent reasonableness. Mira maintained distance; her posture deliberately neutral. Neither showed overt hostility, yet the air between them seemed charged with unspoken tension.

After several minutes of conversation, Michael gestured toward the factory entrance. To Daniel's alarm, Mira followed him inside. This wasn't part of their plan, all discussions were supposed to happen in the open, visible from Daniel's position.

Daniel moved quickly, maintaining cover as he worked his way closer to the main building. As he approached, he heard raised voices echoing from within the cavernous structure. He slipped inside through a side entrance, finding himself in what had once been the factory floor, now a vast, empty space with scattered debris and graffiti-covered walls.

"—never understood what was at stake," Michael was saying, his voice carrying in the empty space. "This was never about money."

"Then what was it about?" Mira's voice controlled but with an underlying edge. "Power? Control?"

"Legacy," Michael replied. "Building something that would outlast all of us. Something worthy of the Voss name."

"By destroying others? By killing Kimberly?"

Michael's laugh echoed off concrete walls. "Such melodrama. Kimberly isn't dead."

Daniel froze behind a partial wall, heart pounding. This was the confirmation they'd been looking for, direct from Michael himself.

"Where is she?" Mira demanded.

"Safe," Michael replied. "And silent, which is what matters. She had the unfortunate habit of asking too many questions about financial arrangements that didn't concern her."

"Like the offshore accounts? The laundered money?"

"Details," Michael dismissed. "Means to an end."

Daniel edged forward, staying in the shadows as he tried to get visual confirmation of their positions. He could see them now, standing about twenty feet apart near the center of the factory floor, Michael with his back to a stairwell that led to the catwalks above, Mira facing him with her hands in her coat pockets.

"Did Martin know?" Mira asked. "About Kimberly?"

"Martin knew exactly what he needed to know," Michael replied. "Nothing more, nothing less. Like you should have. We could have been extraordinary together, the three of us. Instead, you chose..."

"Humanity?" Mira suggested. "Basic decency?"

Michael's expression hardened. "Weakness. You chose weakness, disguised as morality. Just like our father."

"Don't you dare compare me to him," Mira said, a rare flash of genuine anger breaking through her composure.

"Why not? The same sentimentality, the same inability to see the bigger picture..."

"I see the picture perfectly clearly," Mira interrupted. "A brother who murdered our parents, exploited our younger brother, and framed an innocent man to cover his tracks." Her voice remained steady despite the enormity of the accusation. "Did I miss anything?"

Michael's calm façade slipped for a fraction of a second, a momentary flash of something cold and calculating before his expression reset to mild amusement. "Quite a plot you've constructed," he said, taking a step toward her. "Compelling, dramatic. Entirely unprovable."

"The book might disagree," Mira replied. "As might the additional evidence we've assembled."

"Ah yes, the book." Michael's smile didn't reach his eyes. "Your collaboration with Mr. Mercer. How is Daniel? Still lurking nearby, I presume?"

Daniel stilled, realizing Michael had known of his presence all along. "This conversation is between us," Mira said firmly.

"Right, family matters should stay in the family," Michael agreed. "Which is why I've taken the liberty of ensuring our privacy."

Daniel became aware of the movement behind him, a soft footfall on concrete, the subtle shift of a shadow. Before he could react, something struck the back of his head with stunning force. The world tilted, then darkened, his consciousness slipping away to the sound of Mira calling his name.

He awoke to pain, a throbbing headache and the uncomfortable strain of arms secured behind his back. Daniel blinked, clearing slowly to reveal the factory floor from a new perspective. He was sitting on the ground, back against a concrete pillar, wrists bound with what felt like plastic zip ties.

"There he is," Michael's voice came from somewhere to his left. "Rejoining us at last." Daniel turned his head, wincing at the movement, to find Michael standing a few feet away. Mira was kneeling beside him, concern evident in her expression.

"You okay?" she asked quietly.

"Been better," Daniel managed, taking stock of their situation. Beyond Michael stood two men in nondescript dark clothing, security professionals by their stance and alertness.

One held a gun casually at his side. "What happened to our surveillance?"

"Temporarily indisposed," Michael replied. "Nothing personal, simply a necessary precaution. Agent Kwan's team is remarkably dedicated, but somewhat predictable in their approach."

"What do you want, Michael?" Mira asked, standing to face her brother.

"What I've always wanted," he replied simply. "Family cooperation. Unity of purpose."

"That's not going to happen," she said firmly.

Michael sighed, as if disappointed by a child's obstinance. "Then we move to less appealing alternatives." He nodded to one of his men, who produced a tablet and handed it to him. "Your manuscript makes for interesting reading. Quite creative in its interpretation of events."

Daniel felt a chill. "How did you?"

"Access your secure storage?" Michael finished. "Please. Digital security is only as reliable as the humans who implement it. Humans have weaknesses, pressure points."

"What have you done?" Mira demanded.

"Nothing irreversible. Yet." Michael's expression remained pleasant but his eyes had hardened to flint. "The manuscript can be destroyed. The evidence altered or discredited. Even your credibility can be systematically dismantled through carefully placed information."

"You can't silence both of us," Daniel said.

"No?" Michael seemed genuinely amused. "People are silenced every day, Mr. Mercer. Sometimes literally, sometimes through more subtle means. Reputation, career, relationships, all can be destroyed with surgical precision when one has the right tools."

"And Kimberly Renner?" Daniel pressed. "Was she 'silenced' too?"

"She made her choice," Michael replied dismissively. "As you're both about to make yours."

He moved closer, looking between them with calculated assessment. "Option one: you both walk away from this. The manuscript is never published, all copies destroyed. In exchange, you remain unharmed, your lives intact, if somewhat altered. Daniel returns to legitimate journalism, covering topics far removed from financial crimes. Mira relocates—perhaps internationally. I hear Buenos Aires is lovely year-round."

"And option two?" Mira asked, though her tone suggested she already knew.

"Less pleasant," Michael said simply. "For everyone involved." The implied threat hung in the air, made more chilling by Michael's matter-of-fact delivery. Daniel tested his bonds discreetly, finding no give in the plastic restraints.

"You're not walking away from this, Michael," he said with more confidence than he felt. "Too many people know too much."

"People are remarkably susceptible to doubt," Michael countered. "Especially when faced with contradictory evidence from credible sources."

"Such as?" Mira challenged.

Michael smiled. "Such as Martin."

Daniel saw Mira's composure slip for the first time. "What?"

"Our brother had a change of heart before he died," Michael explained. "His diary is there to testify that his earlier statements were made under duress; specifically, pressure from you, Mira, motivated by some misguided vendetta against me."

"That's absurd," she said. "No one would believe"

"They would if accompanied by evidence of your long-standing psychological issues," Michael interrupted. "The therapy records, the medication history, all painting a picture of someone whose perception of reality is... compromised."

Daniel watched Mira's face pale. "You can't access those records. They're protected" "

By privacy laws that become irrelevant with the right connections," Michael finished. "Nothing is truly secure, sister. I thought, I taught you that."

For a terrible moment, Daniel could see Mira wavering, the weight of Michael's threats landing with precision on her most vulnerable points. He struggled against his restraints with renewed urgency.

"Mira," he said firmly, drawing her attention. "He's bluffing. About Martin, about the records, all of it."

"Am I?" Michael raised an eyebrow. "Care to stake your life on that assumption, Mr. Mercer? Or more importantly, hers?"

The security guard shifted his weapon to emphasize the point. Daniel met Mira's gaze, trying to communicate confidence he didn't entirely feel.

"I would," he said steadily. "Because unlike you, Michael, I've actually seen what Mira is capable of. She's stronger than your manipulation, smarter than your threats, and braver than you could ever comprehend."

Michael's expression hardened. "Touching sentiment. Ultimately irrelevant."

"Is it?" Mira's voice had changed; the uncertainty replaced by something cooler, more resolved. "You've never understood, have you, Michael? You're so convinced of your own brilliance that you miss the obvious."

"Which is?" Michael asked a hint of genuine curiosity in his tone.

"That this entire meeting is being recorded," she replied. "Has been from the moment I stepped out of my car."

Michael's smile faltered. "A bluff. My men searched you."

"Not thoroughly enough," Mira replied. She slowly removed her hand from her coat pocket, revealing a small object that Daniel recognized as a recording device disguised as a standard key fob. "Gift from Agent Kwan. Broadcasting directly to an FBI server since activation."

For the first time, Michael appeared genuinely unsettled. "My people disabled all surveillance."

"Standard surveillance, yes," Mira agreed. "But not this prototype. Not when they didn't know to look for it."

The confidence in her voice was absolute, without a trace of the earlier vulnerability. Daniel realized with sudden clarity that he was witnessing the real Mira, neither the calculating woman who had first approached him nor the vulnerable partner of recent days, but a fusion of both: strategic and genuine, determined and compassionate.

"You're lying," Michael said, but doubt had crept into his tone.

"Would you like to test that theory?" Mira challenged. "Your confession about Kimberly Renner is already logged and transmitted. Your threats against us, documented. Your admission about compromising Agent Kwan's team; federal officers, that's a separate charge entirely."

The security men exchanged glances, professional instinct clearly registering the shift in circumstances. Michael's expression darkened.

"Even if that's true," he said carefully, "you're still in a vulnerable position."

"Less vulnerable than you might think," Daniel interjected, noticing movement at the far end of the factory floor. Shadows shifting, figures advancing with practiced stealth.

Michael followed his gaze, expression hardening as he recognized the tactical approach of FBI agents. "Always the contingency plans," he murmured, almost appreciatively. "You learned that from me, at least."

"I learned what not to become," Mira corrected. "There's a difference."

Michael studied her for a long moment, a complex emotion crossing his face, something between respect and regret. Then his expression reset to practiced neutrality.

"Gentlemen," he called to his security team, "I believe our business here is concluded."

What happened next unfolded with dizzying speed. The security men moved toward the rear exit, abandoning their employer without hesitation. Michael reached into his coat, for a weapon, Daniel assumed, but instead withdrew a small remote device.

"Family loyalty above all," Michael said, looking directly at Mira. "Remember that."

He pressed something on the device, then turned and sprinted toward the stairwell. Simultaneous with his movement came a series of sharp cracks from different points in the factory, small explosions that sent concrete dust billowing through the space.

"Diversionary charges," Mira explained, dropping to her knees beside Daniel and producing a small knife from her boot to cut his restraints. "Non-lethal but effective. Classic Michael."

"We need to go after him," Daniel said as she freed his hands.

"The FBI will," she replied, helping him to his feet. "Our priority is getting out before...."

A larger explosion shook the building, this one structural rather than diversionary. Part of the catwalk above came crashing down, blocking the main entrance to the factory floor. Smoke began filling the space, acrid and disorienting.

"This way," Mira ordered, pulling Daniel toward a side exit he hadn't noticed before. "The building won't hold much longer."

They moved through smoke and falling debris, Mira navigating with surprising confidence given the chaotic conditions. Behind them, the sound of pursuit suggested the FBI team was still in the building, though whether pursuing them or Michael remained unclear.

They burst through a rusted door into the winter air, the temperature shock nearly as stunning as the contrast between smoky interior and clear night. The sun had fully set during their confrontation, leaving the factory grounds illuminated only by emergency vehicle lights now converging on the property.

"Keep moving," Mira urged, guiding Daniel toward a stand of trees at the perimeter.

"We should check in with Kwan," he objected, though he continued following her lead.

"After we're clear," she insisted. "Michael planned this too carefully for it to end so simply."

As if confirming her assessment, another explosion rocked the main factory building, this one more substantial than the others. The roof partially collapsed, sending a plume of dust and smoke into the night sky. Emergency vehicles swerved to avoid falling debris, their paths illuminated in the harsh emergency lights.

Daniel and Mira reached the tree line, where they paused, catching their breath as they surveyed the chaos behind them. FBI agents were establishing a perimeter, tactical teams deploying with practiced efficiency. There was no sign of Michael or his security team.

"Do you think he got away?" Daniel asked, wincing as pain from his earlier head wound reasserted itself.

Mira's expression was complicated; relief mixed with something harder to identify. "For now. But his options are limited. The recording, the FBI witnesses, he can't simply return to business as usual."

"What did he mean about family loyalty?" Daniel asked, remembering Michael's final words.

Before Mira could answer, her phone vibrated. She checked it, her face paling in the blue-white light of the screen.

"What is it?" Daniel asked.

"A message," she said quietly. "From Michael."

She turned the phone so Daniel could see. "Family business remains unfinished. Martin chose his side. Will you choose yours?"

Daniel felt cold that had nothing to do with the winter night. "Is that..."

"A threat," Mira confirmed. "And a final play for control." She took a deep breath, her expression hardening with resolve. "But he's miscalculated. Again."

She dialed Agent Kwan directly, quickly explaining the situation. Within minutes, arrangements were being made for her and Daniel’s protection and a new search for Michael initiated. When she ended the call, Mira turned to Daniel with grim determination.

"It's not over," she said simply.

"No," Daniel agreed, looking at the burning factory behind them, a fitting metaphor for the destruction Michael left in his wake. "But for the first time, I think we're ahead of him rather than behind."

Mira's hand found him in the darkness, her grip firm and certain. "The manuscript?"

"Safe," Daniel assured her. "Multiple backups, multiple locations."

"Then we finish this," she said. "On our terms, not his."

They stood together at the edge of the tree line, watching as emergency crews fought to contain the factory fire. Michael had escaped immediate capture, but at the cost of further incriminating himself. The evidence against him was mounting, his options diminishing with every calculated risk.

As they made their way back toward the perimeter to connect with Agent Kwan, Daniel felt a strange clarity despite the chaos of the evening. Their book would be published. Michael would eventually be caught. Justice, however imperfect, would be served.

But it was the woman beside him, complex, resilient, and finally liberated from her brother's manipulations, who represented the true victory. Mira had faced her demons and emerged stronger, her fragmented self-coalescing into something whole and formidable.

CHAPTER 13: RESOLUTION

The aftermath of the factory confrontation unfolded with unexpected swiftness. Michael remained at large for exactly forty-seven hours before being apprehended at a private airfield outside Toronto, attempting to board a chartered plane to Venezuela. His escape plans, meticulous as they were, had been compromised by the very thing he consistently underestimated: human connection.

"It was his pilot," Agent Kwan explained, seated across from Daniel and Mira in a secure FBI conference room. "They'd worked together for years, but Michael made a crucial error."

"He threatened the man's family," Mira said. It wasn't a question.

Kwan nodded. "Implied harm if the departure wasn't expedited. The pilot contacted us immediately."

"Michael never understood the difference between fear and loyalty," Mira observed quietly.

Three days after Michael's arrest, they submitted the final manuscript to the publisher. The book, titled The Architecture of Deception: Inside a Master Manipulator's Mind, was fast-tracked for publication. Security measures were made in place to protect both the content and its authors.

As winter yielded to early spring, preparations for Michael's trial intensified. The prosecution's case had strengthened considerably following his documented threats and attempted flight.

More significantly, Kimberly Renner had been located alive, hidden in plain sight as a psychiatric patient in a private facility outside Seattle. She was committed under a false identity with documentation suggesting paranoid delusions.

"She's still traumatized," Agent Kwan reported after the initial interview. "But coherent. Her testimony will be devastating to Michael's defense."

The lead-up to publication brought unexpected challenges. Michael's remaining allies attempted last-minute legal maneuvers to suppress the book, claiming defamation and interference with ongoing judicial proceedings.

When these failed, more direct methods emerged, veiled threats to the publishing team, suspicious activity around Daniel's apartment, and a break-in attempt at Mira's new residence.

Through it all, Daniel and Mira maintained their focus, navigating the complex terrain of their professional partnership and personal relationship with cautious determination. The intensity of their shared experience had created a bond that defied conventional definition, deeper than collaboration, more nuanced than romance, though elements of both existed within it.

"We should talk about what happens after," Daniel said one evening as they reviewed final proofs in his apartment. The book's release was scheduled for the following week, coinciding with the beginning of jury selection for Michael's trial.

"After what?" Mira asked, though her tone suggested she understood perfectly.

"After publication. After the trial." Daniel hesitated. "After all this is finally behind us."

Mira set aside the page she'd been reviewing. "You assume there will be an 'after.'"

"There usually is," he replied with a small smile. "That's how time works."

"Very profound," she said dryly, but her expression softened. "What exactly are you asking, Daniel?"

He considered her words carefully, maintaining the balance they'd established in recent weeks, but found himself unwilling to perpetuate uncertainty.

"I'm asking what you want," he said simply. "From your life. From..." He gestured between them. "This."

Mira was quiet for a long moment, her gaze drifting to the window where spring rain tapped a gentle rhythm against the glass. "I've spent most of my life reacting," she finally said. "To Michael's manipulations, to family trauma, to circumstances beyond my control. I'm not sure I know how to want things proactively."

"You wanted to stop Michael," Daniel pointed out. "You wanted to tell the truth in this book."

"Reaction and response," she countered. "Different faces of the same coin."

"Then maybe it's time to flip the coin," Daniel suggested. "See what's on the other side."

Mira studied him with an expression he'd come to recognize, assessment blended with something more vulnerable.

"What do you want, Daniel?" she asked, turning his question back on him. He'd been expecting this, had prepared a measured response that acknowledged the complexity of their situation while leaving space for multiple possibilities. Instead, he found himself answering with simple honesty.

"You," he said. "However, that works. Whatever shape it takes."

The admission hung between them, more exposed than he'd intended. Mira didn't respond immediately, and Daniel felt a momentary flash of regret at his directness.

"Sorry," he began. "That was..."

"Honest," she interrupted. "It was honest." She reached the table and covered his hand with hers. "I'm not very good at that when it comes to emotions. But I'm learning."

Before Daniel could respond, his phone rang with Agent Kwan's distinctive tone. He answered, listening intently for several minutes before thanking her and ending the call.

"What is it?" Mira asked, recognizing the significance in his expression.

"Michael's attorney has approached the prosecution with a plea deal," Daniel explained. "Reduced charges in exchange for information about financial crimes involving several high-profile business associates."

"He's sacrificing others to save himself," Mira observed.

"Apparently." Daniel set his phone down. "Kwan says the prosecution is considering it, given the scope of the additional cases they could build.

“Will they drop the charges related to Kimberly?"

Daniel shook his head. "Those remain non-negotiable. The best case for Michael is still substantial prison time, just not life."

Mira absorbed this information with complicated emotions visible in her expression, relief, vindication, and something that might have been sorrow for what her brother had become. "So, it's almost over," she said quietly.

"This part, at least," Daniel agreed.

She looked at him then with unexpected clarity. "To answer your question," she said, "what I want is to stop defining my life in relation to Michael. To discover who I am without his shadow. And" she hesitated, then continued with determined honesty, "I'd like to do that with you. If that's still what you want."

Daniel felt something expand in his chest, hope, possibility, future. "It is," he assured her. Mira's smile was cautious but genuine.

"Then I suppose we'll have to figure out what that looks like."

"Together," Daniel suggested.

"Together," she agreed.

They returned to the proofs, working in comfortable silence as rain continued to fall outside. The road ahead remained uncertain, Michael's legal proceedings, the book's reception, their own evolving relationship, but for the first time, uncertainty felt like possibility rather than threat.

The final pages of the manuscript contained a conclusion they had written together, its closing paragraph a testament to the journey they had shared:

Truth is rarely convenient and never simple. It exists in layers, revealed gradually through persistent questioning and honest examination. In exposing Michael Voss's architecture of deception, we discovered that true justice isn't merely about punishment for past wrongs, but about creating space for future healing, for his victims, for those unwittingly drawn into his orbit, and perhaps most importantly, for ourselves.

Some stories end with neat resolution, all questions answered, all loose ends tied. This is not one of those stories. But perhaps the most valuable narratives are those that remain somewhat open, inviting continued reflection and growth beyond the final page.

The book's release occurred on a bright Tuesday in April. By Wednesday afternoon, it had reached the top of multiple bestseller lists, its revelations sparking intense media coverage and renewed scrutiny of white-collar crime prosecution. By Friday, they had received requests for interviews from every major news outlet in the country.

"We should be selective," Daniel advised as they reviewed the growing list of inquiries. "Focus on substantive discussions rather than sensationalism."

Mira nodded, sorting requests into categories. "Agreed. And we should be prepared for backlash from Michael's allies."

"The publisher's security team is monitoring threats," Daniel assured her. "And Kwan says the FBI is keeping tabs on anyone with a motive to retaliate."

Despite these precautions, they maintained vigilance in the weeks following publication. Michael's extensive network meant potential danger from unexpected directions. But as May turned to June with no significant incidents, they gradually adjusted to their new reality, authors of a bestselling exposé, key witnesses in a high-profile trial, and increasingly, partners in a relationship that defied norms.

Daniel's journalism career had been revitalized, with offers coming from publications that had previously rejected his pitches. Mira received inquiries about consulting on cases involving psychological manipulation and financial fraud. Both approached these opportunities with cautious interest, aware that their futures were still taking shape.

On the anniversary of their first meeting, a date neither of them had consciously tracked but both somehow remembered, they returned to the coffee shop where Daniel had once waited with suspicion for the subject of his book.

"Strange to think how it began," he remarked as they claimed a table near the window, the same one he had occupied a year earlier.

"With deception," Mira noted, wrapping her hands around her mug.

"And ended with truth," Daniel added.

She smiled; the expression more natural now than it had been months ago. "Is this an ending?"

"No," Daniel conceded. "More like a milestone."

They sat in comfortable silence, watching afternoon light filter through new spring leaves. Outside, the city continued its relentless pace, unchanged by their personal journey yet somehow different through the lens of their shared experience.

"I received a letter from Michael yesterday," Mira said eventually. "His first direct communication since the arrest."

Daniel's expression sharpened with concern. "What did he say?"

"Very little of substance. Philosophical musings about family, legacy, the nature of truth." She shrugged slightly. "Classic Michael, reframing his situation as somehow transcendent rather than criminal."

"Are you going to respond?"

Mira considered this. "I haven't decided. Part of me thinks any response continues the cycle. Another part recognizes he's still my brother, despite everything."

"What does he want from you?" Daniel asked.

"Forgiveness, perhaps," she replied. "Or more likely, acknowledgment. Michael has always needed to be the center of everyone's life."

"And is he? Still the center of yours?"

Mira reached the table, taking Daniel's hand in a gesture that had become familiar between them.

"No," she said with quiet certainty. "Not anymore."

Outside, afternoon drifted toward evening, the city transitioning from workday to nightlife. Inside, they remained at their table, talking about possibilities that had nothing to do with Michael Voss or criminal investigations. They discussed about the places they might enjoy, books they wanted to read, and the small apartment they were considering sharing when Daniel's lease ended in August.

Sometimes Daniel's mind went to whatever happened at Mira's house that night. She said that she had not drugged him that day. Was that the truth? Had he actually had too much wine to create situations in his mind which were not true. Yet with his growing closeness with Mira, he had stopped thinking about that night and the loopholes in his memory.

As they eventually left the coffee shop, stepping into the gentle evening air, Daniel felt a sense of completion that had nothing to do with cases closed or published books. It existed in the woman beside him, in the trust they had earned from each other, in the future they were choosing to explore together.

Some stories ended with neat resolution, all questions answered, all loose ends tied. This was not one of those stories. But perhaps the most valuable stories were those that remained somewhat open, inviting continued reflection and growth beyond the final page.

EPILOGUE

Mira stood at the window of her new apartment, watching early morning light transform the city skyline. Behind her, Daniel slept peacefully, unaware of her predawn restlessness. This happened occasionally, waking in darkness, a mind active with memories she usually kept carefully contained.

Today marked one year since Michael's sentencing. Eighteen years with the possibility of parole after twelve, less than the prosecution had sought, more than the defense had hoped for. Mira had attended every day of the trial, watching her brother's performance gradually crumble under the weight of accumulated evidence and testimony.

She turned from the window, making her way silently to the kitchen to prepare coffee. As water heated, she found herself retrieving the small lockbox she kept in her office drawer; a collection of items she rarely examined but couldn't bring herself to discard.

The box contained remnants of her former self, preserved like artifacts from an archaeological dig: a worn leather-bound notebook filled with observations and strategies from her years working alongside Michael.

There were several identity documents under various names; a flash drive containing contingency plans never activated; a single photograph of herself, Michael, and Martin taken at their parents' funeral, their expressions inappropriately composed given the circumstances.

Mira spread these items on the kitchen counter, studying them with clinical detachment. The woman who had collected these things seemed simultaneously familiar and foreign, a version of herself constructed for survival, shaped by Michael's influence and her own adaptability.

That woman had done things the current Mira preferred not to dwell on. Small betrayals at first, information gathering through manipulated relationships, strategic deceptions that served the siblings' financial interests. Later, more significant transgressions, evidence altered or removed, potential witnesses intimidated or compromised, ethical boundaries not just crossed but obliterated.

She had been good at it. That was the truth she had never fully shared with Daniel, though he had likely intuited it. For years, she had operated as Michael's most effective lieutenant, her psychological training providing insights that made their operations nearly undetectable. While Michael planned, Mira implemented, identifying vulnerabilities, establishing trust, extracting what was needed before disappearing from her targets' lives.

There had been men like Daniel before, intelligent, principled, genuinely good people whose paths intersected with the Voss siblings' schemes. Men she had approached with altered personas designed specifically for them. Their trust she had cultivated with practiced precision, only to desert them when the job was done.

She had drugged him that night and blatantly denied doing it. In fact, she was surprised Daniel had never questioned her again about it. What a naïve man he was? Mira had subjected him to mental trauma which he might not get over, ever in this life. The same trauma that her little brother Martin had experienced after Daniel's book released. His confused state when he came back to her home was priceless, just what she craved to see.

Yet, there had been something different with Daniel? What was it? Mira had asked herself this question repeatedly over the past year. Was it Martin's deterioration and suicide that had finally forced her to confront the consequences of their actions? Was it the realization that Michael had been manipulating her as thoroughly as she had manipulated others? Or was it something in Daniel himself, an integrity that had refused to be corrupted?

Perhaps all of this, she acknowledged, closing the notebook that contained strategies she had once employed without hesitation. Her approach to Daniel had begun as standard procedure, establish connection, build trust, extract information etc. But somewhere in the process, the script had faltered, authenticity bleeding into performance until the boundaries blurred beyond recognition.

The coffee maker beeped softly, pulling Mira from her reflections. As she poured a cup, she heard movement from the bedroom, Daniel waking, going through his own morning routine. She quickly returned the items to their box, hesitating over the photograph before including it as well.

"Morning," Daniel greeted her minutes later, hair tousled from sleep. He kissed her cheek before pouring his own coffee. "You're up early."

"Couldn't sleep," she replied with a small smile.

"Thinking about the anniversary." Daniel nodded, understanding immediately.

"One year since sentencing. How are you feeling about it?"

This was what continued to surprise her about him, the directness of his questions, the assumption that her emotions were valid regardless of their complexity. "Conflicted," she admitted. "Relief that it's over, that he can't hurt anyone else. But also...

"He's still your brother," Daniel finished when she hesitated.

"Yes." She took a sip of coffee. "And I'm still the person who worked beside him for years.

Who participated in what he did."

Daniel leaned against the counter, studying her with the thoughtful attention that had initially disarmed her defenses.

"You know what is the difference between you and Michael?" he asked.

Mira raised an eyebrow, waiting.

"You recognize the harm," Daniel said simply. "You feel it. It matters to you."

"That doesn't erase what I did," she pointed out.

"No," he agreed. "But it's why you stopped. Why you helped bring him to justice despite the personal cost. Why you've spent the past year working on bringing out the truth."

This was true. In the aftermath of the trial, Mira had established a foundation for those affected by white-collar crime, providing both practical resources and psychological support. The work was challenging but essential to her own healing process, the form of restitution that acknowledged her part in similar harms.

"I'm not seeking absolution," Mira said quietly.

"I know." Daniel set down his coffee and moved closer, his hand finding hers on the counter. "That's not what this is about."

"What is it about then?" she asked, genuinely curious about his perspective.

"Integration," he replied thoughtfully. "Accepting all parts of yourself, the person you were, the person you are, the person you're becoming. Not compartmentalizing or denying, but acknowledging and learning."

Mira felt something in her chest loosen at his words. This was why she had fallen in love with Daniel Mercer, not his forgiveness or acceptance, but his insistence on whole truth, even when uncomfortable. Especially when uncomfortable.

"When did you get so wise?" she asked with a small smile.

"Around the time I fell in love with a complicated woman who keeps making me reconsider everything I thought I knew," he replied, returning her smile with his own.

The morning light had strengthened, illuminating the apartment they now shared. Outside, the city was fully awake, its rhythms unaffected by personal revelations or private reconciliations. Within these walls, however, something significant had shifted, not dramatically, but in the subtle way of genuine growth.

Mira felt the shift as she moved through their morning routine, shower, breakfast, preparation for the day ahead. The memories and artifacts of her former self remained, acknowledged rather than denied. The woman she had been existed alongside the woman she was becoming, neither negating the other but creating something more integrated, more authentic.

Later that day, as she met with a new client at the foundation, a former employee of one of Michael's associates who had unwittingly participated in fraudulent activities, Mira recognized her unique qualification for this work. Her experience as both perpetrator and victim allowed her to navigate complex terrain others might simplify or misunderstand.

"You can move forward without erasing what happened," she told the young woman sitting across from her, distress evident in her posture. "It becomes part of your story, but not its definition."

As she spoke these words, Mira realized she was finally beginning to believe them herself.

That evening, she and Daniel walked along the riverfront, comfortable in conversation and silence alike. When they passed the gleaming financial district where Michael had once operated with seeming impunity, Mira felt a momentary shadow, not of his influence, but of recognition for how thoroughly their lives had been transformed.

"Penny for your thoughts?" Daniel asked, noting her expression.

Mira considered retorting with something lighter, an old habit of self-protection. Instead, she opted for honesty. "I was thinking about parallel lives," she said. "The one I might be living if I'd stayed on Michael's path. The one I'm living now."

Daniel nodded, understanding as always. "Any regrets about your choice?" "About leaving Michael's world?

No." She squeezed his hand gently. "About how long it took me to make that choice? Many."

"We can't change timing," Daniel observed. "Only direction."

"Another profound statement," Mira teased. "Should I be attributing these in the second edition of our book?"

He laughed, the sound warming her despite the evening chill. "I think I'll leave the in-depth insights to you. I'm just figuring things out as we go."

"Aren't we all," she agreed. They continued their walk as twilight settled over the city, streetlights illuminating their path forward. Mira felt the weight of the past, its shadows and complexities, still present but no longer defining. Ahead lay uncertainty, but also possibility, connection, growth.

The woman who had once calculated every interaction for maximum advantage now found herself embracing experiences without predetermined outcomes. The architect of manipulation had become a builder of something more enduring, trust, authenticity, love freely given and received.

It wasn't redemption, exactly. Some actions couldn't be redeemed, only acknowledged and learned from. But it was transformation, deliberate and ongoing, imperfect but genuine.

Walking home with Daniel as night fell, Mira realized the biggest difference between her and Michael: she could change and break old habits, but he couldn't.

The streetlights flickered one by one, casting long shadows across their path. Daniel's hand found her in the darkness, his touch warm and steady. She squeezed back, grateful for his presence beside her.

Michael would always be Michael, stuck in the same patterns, making the same mistakes, refusing to see beyond his own limited perspective. For years, she had believed she was just like him, destined to repeat the cycles of her past. How many nights had she lain awake, terrified that she would never escape the person she had been?

But here she was, walking a different path. The choice had been hers all along.

"You okay?" Daniel asked, noticing her silence.

Mira nodded, looking up at the first stars appearing in the evening sky. "Just thinking about how far I've come," she said.

As they turned onto their street, the porch light of their small house glowed in the distance like a beacon. Home. Not just a place, but a promise. A beginning.

"We should plant those flowers this weekend," she said, nodding toward their empty garden beds as they approached.

Daniel smiled. "Planning for next season already?"

"Why not?" Mira said, her voice stronger than she expected. "I want to see what grows."

She paused at their front steps, taking one last look at the night sky before going inside. The stars continued their ancient patterns overhead, unchanging in their courses. But down here, beneath their distant light, Mira had discovered something intense: the courage to change, to grow beyond what once seemed inescapable.

And in that discovery, she had finally found herself.

Her brother remained confined by his own architecture of deception, unable to imagine existence beyond its calculated parameters. Mira had found her way out, step by uncertain step, into a less controlled life but infinitely more authentic.

The past would always be part of her story. But for the first time, it didn't determine the chapters yet to be written.

Manufactured by Amazon.ca
Bolton, ON

55376951R00055